Tournament Games

A Zimbell House Anthology

Tournament Games

A Zimbell House Anthology

For permission requests, write to the publisher at the address below:
"Attention: Permissions Coordinator"
Zimbell House Publishing, LLC
PO Box 1172
Union Lake, Michigan 48387
mail to: info@zimbellhousepublishing.com

© 2016 Zimbell House Publishing, LLC
Cover Design by The Book Planners
www.TheBookPlanners.com

Published in the United States by Zimbell House Publishing
http://www.ZimbellHousePublishing.com
All Rights Reserved

Print ISBN: 978-1-942818-80-9
Kindle ISBN: 978-1-942818-81-6
Digital ISBN: 978-1-945967-14-6
Trade Paper ISBN: 978-1-945967-52-8
Library of Congress Control Number: 2016908953

First Edition: June 2016
10 9 8 7 6 5 4

Acknowledgements

Zimbell House Publishing would like to thank all those that contributed to this anthology. We chose to showcase six unique writers to entertain us with seven fictional tales from the middle ages.

Zimbell House would also like to thank our team, without their hard work and dedication, these anthologies would not exist.

A special thank you goes out to The Book Planners for yet another great cover design.

Contents

Jousting for Murder

Sammi Cox

The horse's hooves thundered, raising clods of earth from the ground with each stride. Although there were only two horses, each dressed to match the rider they were carrying, the noise seemed deafening.

That was until the riders collided and their lances smashed upon the other, sending splinters of wood flying through the air. One rider kept his seat, although the impact knocked him backwards. Slowly, no doubt due to the weight of the armour as well as the strike to his person, he righted himself as the horse slowed down before turning to face the lists once more.

Only then did he, Miles Chevalier, realise that he was the only one to keep his seat. His opponent, his own brother Will, lay sprawled across the ground, unmoving.

Where before the sound of the tourney echoed across the northern bank of the river, now there was only silence and stillness. All eyes were on the motionless body. No-one moved but the riderless horse.

Panic surged through the cloud of shock which had overcome the winner. He dropped his reins, raised his visor and scanned the gathering of stewards, men-at-arms, squires and grooms.

"To me!" he screamed, knowing full well he couldn't get off his horse unaided.

Those words seemed to awaken the crowd. All at once, noise erupted, and people began moving.

His men were beside him in a flash, pulling him from his saddle. Pain exploded in his shoulder. Gritting his teeth against the terrible agony, he glanced down, just this minute realising he was wounded. Blood oozed from a small puncture hole, dribbling down his armour like red rivulets.

"You're wounded, sire," one of the squires exclaimed, as another removed his helmet. But he was disinterested in his own injury; he needed to get to his brother.

Pushing men out of his way, he stumbled back to where a crowd had gathered around the still figure of Will.

Muttering a silent prayer to God and all the saints, he cleared a little space and fell to his knees. As he pulled his brother's helm from his head, he realised that it would take more than prayers to wake him now. It was obvious for all to see. His brother was dead.

As Miles took in the bruised and bloodied face of his brother, a roar escaped his lips. Someone tried to pull him away and got a fist full of mail for his efforts. Another man tried instead to move the dead body, so Miles drew his sword. Pain flared through the muscle in his shoulder. Numbly he seemed to recall that he had been wounded and now lacked the power to wield such a heavy blade.

His sword fell from his grasp, but it didn't matter. In this condition it was useless. He needed something lighter, something that wouldn't strain him as much. He pulled a dagger from its sheath and levelled it at the circle of men, who had instinctively taken a step backward.

From the corner of his eye, he could see the stands emptying of people, though the Baron with his entourage remained where they were, looking on. Dimly Miles registered that it was the Baron's birthday, the joust having been staged in his honour. However, there would be no more celebrating now. Miles and Will had grown up in the company of the Baron. They had trained together, learned to ride the great warhorses together and how to handle sword, dagger, and mace. They were friends.

But none of that was important. Will was dead. Guilt erupted inside of him. Even as he saw the vivid, blotchy colours marking his brother's face, knowing that such wounds were not the result of the joust and were hours old, he couldn't help but think himself to blame. For surely, that was what everyone was thinking; Miles Chevalier had slain his own brother in front of the lists.

Nausea threatened to overwhelm him. Blood pounded in his ears, a noise not dissimilar to the sound of hooves striking the earth.

"My lord," someone called out to him. He had no idea who or even from which side they came from. Things were descending into a blur, but he tried to fight against it, to remain in control. It was much easier said than done.

He glanced down at Will once more, hoping to find the strength he needed to go on. Unfortunately, that was not the case. As he took in the dull, lifeless eyes, staring without seeing at the sky above them, he felt worse.

His head was whirling uncontrollably, a tempest of bloody images and silent accusations. Suddenly, remaining upright seemed impossible. As his vision slowly dimmed, he felt the world fall away. He was already unconscious when his body struck the ground with a dull thud.

When Miles woke, it was to the sight of long rays of sunlight streaming in through a small, high window. Groggily, he looked around, his head feeling uncomfortable and heavier than he remembered. He quickly realised that moving, even a little, was not a good idea. A burning sensation flared in his shoulder and dizziness threatened.

"That will be the poppy," a soft voice said, his tone sounding as if he had just been roused from sleep. A long, lazy yawn followed. "Lie back down, Miles. You're not yet healed."

Gentle hands eased him backward. A face loomed above him. "John?" he asked, noticing the man's attire. Miles thought he recognised him but was unsure. He was wearing the coarse robes of a monk.

"Ah, you remember me now. Though you seem to have forgotten that it's Brother John and has been for a number of years. Never mind, progress is progress. For two days you've had no idea who I was."

Miles's brow wrinkled in confusion, "Two days?"

"It doesn't matter, not yet," Brother John told him, sitting alongside him. "You must rest."

But Miles couldn't. Something on the edge of his awareness told him that there was a serious matter that required his attention, but the poppy made it difficult to grasp what it was.

"Don't fight it, Miles. Just go back to sleep. When it wears off, we will talk."

Miles closed his eyes. Seeing John, no, *Brother* John, brought to mind scenes from childhood, when they were all studying at the Abbey, learning to read and write. There was Hugh, Will, and John and himself, of course. John was now a monk at the same abbey that had educated them, whilst Hugh had become the Baron de Witton.

As these distant recollections played over in his muddled mind, an urgent niggling continued to press upon him. He went over the names of his friends again. Baron Hugh de Witton. Brother John. His flesh and blood brother, Will.

Then images dark and disturbing returned to him. He gasped. His eyes shot open.

"Miles? What is it?" John asked, stumbling to his feet.

"Will. Where is Will?"

The look on John's face told Miles that this was not the horrific nightmare induced by the poppy he had been given.

Miles nodded. "Where is he?" he asked again, though this time his question was different. The first time he had been asking why his brother was not at his bedside. The second was to inquire after his body.

"Laid out in the chapel."

Again, Miles nodded. Exhaustion threatened to overwhelm him, but he needed to finish what he had to say. His eyelids began to droop, and though his words came, they were much slower than normal. "Go to him, John. Check him over. Will was murdered. I know it…I know it…"

After the final word had been uttered, Miles fell into the deep darkness of poppy sleep.

The next time Miles stirred it was to find the room blanketed in darkness, except for the soft glow of a brazier. The seat Brother John had earlier occupied was empty.

He drifted back off into an unsettled, restless sleep, but on hearing the sound of footsteps approaching, woke once more.

"You are awake, my friend?" John whispered, leaning over him. Miles nodded. The look on John's face gave him cause for concern. "I have just returned from what you asked of me." He paused, waiting to see if Miles remembered. How could he forget? John continued. "I think you're right. Someone went to task on Will. If I had to guess, your brother was already dead when he was unhorsed, not long before it perhaps, but dead nonetheless. You didn't kill Will, Miles. But someone else did and from the look of him, they wanted to make sure that he didn't wake up. Underneath the bruises, I found a stab wound and a skull fracture."

Hearing John's verdict, Miles remained surprisingly calm and knew what he must do. "I need to speak with Hugh, John. Help me to my feet." He was still unsteady as he tried to swing his legs off the bed, but he couldn't delay. To his mind, he had already wasted enough time lying in bed whilst his brother's murderer remained free.

"You want to go now? It's the middle of the night, Miles. And how am I supposed to get you from the abbey to the castle? You can barely stand. What's more, I am forbidden from leaving the abbey confines without the Abbot's permission, as you well know. It will have to wait until morning."

Reluctantly, Miles acknowledged his friend was right.

When morning came, the dilemma solved itself. On hearing that Miles Chevalier was awake and talking, Baron Hugh de Witton came to the infirmary to speak with his friend. In his wake followed a number of attendants and squires, who stood a little way apart to allow the men to talk.

"Sorry about Will," the Baron said, seating himself in John's empty chair. John was now in the abbey church, celebrating the divine office of Terce. "And for such an accident to fall on my birthday."

"It was no accident," Miles corrected him.

Hugh looked sad and weary. "Men are killed and maimed in tournaments all the time, Miles. Why should this loss, sad as it may be to us, be any different?"

"Did you not see his face? He looked like he had been in a tavern brawl, not a joust."

"What are you saying?"

"I did not kill my brother by accident, Hugh. Someone else murdered him. Intentionally."

The accusation caused all conversation in the room to stop abruptly. Sympathetic looks were sent his way.

"I understand-"

"Forgive me, my lord, but you do not."

There was a pause and then a sigh. "Leave us," the Baron bellowed. The room quickly emptied and they were left alone. Hugh rubbed his hands across his face vigorously. Miles thought that his friend looked to be under a great deal of stress. "Explain to me your reasoning. I would understand your thoughts in this. An accusation of murder cannot rest on a split lip and a black eye."

"I would agree if those were the only injuries. John has looked him over. Will was beaten, stabbed and cracked on the head."

"What?" Hugh hissed. "When? With such damage afflicted upon his person, how could he sit on his horse, Miles?"

"It was staged. Don't ask me how, but John believes he was already dead before he was put on the horse."

"Impossible!"

Miles raised his eyebrows. Although his head hurt far less than it had hitherto, there was still a dull ache behind his eyes. He did his best to ignore it. "Unlikely and unexpected…perhaps. But impossible? No. Will arrived late to the lists. I didn't get a chance to speak with him. Did you?"

"No," the Baron growled. He got to his feet and began pacing the length of the small room. It was clear that he was deep in thought, mulling something over. Eventually, he stopped marching and turned to look at Miles. "There is something I need to tell you. But you're not going to like it."

A coldness settled over Miles. Hugh was never particularly fond of sharing what he knew, even with his own trusted men. So, for him to choose to impart something of consequence, now of all times, could only mean that the thing was not to be relished.

"Will had been gone from the town for a few days before my birthday tourney," the Baron began.

"Yes, I know. To Northampton, he said."

"No. That was only a ruse. I sent him to London. To the King. He was supposed to return a few days ago, only for some reason I couldn't fathom, he was delayed. I had instructed him to send word once he reached the King, but I heard nothing."

"Why was he to go to the King? What could be so urgent?"

Even now Hugh was reluctant to reveal the information. Miles could tell that he was wondering if this knowledge was what had got Will killed. Finally, he whispered, "I had heard of a plot to kidnap the prince."

Whatever errand of import he was expecting the Baron to utter, it certainly wasn't that. "Treason!" Miles exclaimed, shocked. "But why would anyone want the prince? He is but a child."

"To bargain with, of course, though for what purpose I do not know. Their intention in doing so was never disclosed to me. Will was with me when I received the news and volunteered to go. He was my fastest rider, and he was loyal to the crown."

"Well, it seems that someone who wasn't found out that he knew and was about to reveal all to the King." Miles sighed. Things were far more complicated than he realised. "Come, sit down, Hugh. You must tell me all. Only then can we begin to understand what befell Will on the road to London."

The Baron did as he was bid, and was soon unburdening himself.

An unknown messenger had arrived unexpectedly at the castle a week ago, begging a private audience with the Baron. The only person present during this was Will, as Hugh had been loathe to empty his hall completely on the say-so of the stranger. These were dangerous times, and it was better to be overly cautious rather than arrogant.

When the messenger realised that the Baron was not going to send Will away, he reluctantly recited the message he had been given:

"Time and again, the King's word has been given on certain matters and each time, without fail, he has reneged upon it. If a King's word cannot be trusted, neither can the King who pledged it. He must be made to see that even a King is not beyond reproach. A princely ransom is what we seek."

"Very clever," Miles had commented once the Baron had completed telling his tale. "Reciting the message so that no evidence of treason ever existed. Neither do they openly declare their intention in the message, instead hiding their dark purpose beneath the words spoken. Is there anything about this messenger that you can remember? What about who sent him?"

"I do not know on whose business he was, Miles. You know how these things work. No names. But the messenger had a memorable face. A scar sliced it in two." Hugh described the man in as much detail as he could. Average height, average build, was probably a soldier once, but not for some years, the Baron guessed. He had unkempt dark hair, though was surprisingly clean-shaven. But it was the scar that ran red and raw, though it had healed, from the left side of his forehead down towards the bottom of his right ear that was his most distinguishing feature, the one they could identify him from.

Miles smiled to himself. *Even I would know him now.*

Once the Baron had left, Miles took to thinking over all he had learnt whilst confined to his sickbed. He knew what had happened to Will had been no accident, and the reason for it had now almost certainly been revealed by Hugh.

The messenger had obviously been dispatched to determine from where their traitorous faction could garner support and perhaps even assistance in their treasonous business. And yet, once he had delivered his message to the Baron de Witton, he had not left to go and deliver it elsewhere. Rather, to have known that Will had been sent to London indicated that he had remained in the town, watching, waiting for a reaction from the Baron. Knowing Will's face, he must have recognised him as he set off on the London road and guessed his purpose.

The 'how' and 'why' of the murder had been easy to explain, now that he was in full possession of the facts. But why go to the effort of waiting until the Baron's birthday tournament before returning Will's body? Why bother getting him into his armour and up on his horse? What was the point of it?

Well, Miles mused, he had plenty of time to think about it, forbidden as he was by the Infirmarian from getting up and exhausting himself. And think about it he would. As soon as he was able, he wanted to track down the scar-faced messenger and settle this outstanding debt.

Miles came to the conclusion that Will had been used to make a point. The day had been carefully chosen—it was no secret that the Baron was celebrating his birthday with a tournament, and the town had been filled with many faces, both familiar and unfamiliar, from the town and further afield. It would not have been hard to slip in and out of the crowd, just one more stranger in town to watch the contests.

Hugh de Witton returned later that day to speak once more with Miles. It was clear that he had been able to think of Will's murder and little else.

"Tell me what you've come up with. I know you've not been sitting idly here," the Baron boomed as he entered. "You know, if their ploy had worked we would not be looking beyond the tournament ground for the culprit."

Miles explained his thoughts to Hugh, who sat on the edge of the seat, avidly listening. Every now and then, he would make a sound that indicated he agreed with his Knight's reasoning, but other than that, he remained silent.

"From what we know to be true, I would guess two things. The first is that whoever was responsible wanted everyone, including you, to see the dead body. The second is that they wanted me to be held accountable for Will's death, at least publicly. You would know why he had died but everyone else would not. Accident or no, it would look like I killed him." Miles didn't say that until he had removed Will's helmet and seen his bloodied and broken face, he thought he had. Those few minutes of guilt would stay with him for the rest of his life.

"So they killed Will to threaten me? To buy my silence?"

"And perhaps to show you how strong they are."

"Well, we shall see about that," the Baron huffed. "They think to make me cower after they killed my friend? I do not bend to cowards."

"And Will wouldn't want you to."

"We will get justice for Will, Miles. That I promise. Now I must go to London myself and speak with the King." Hugh stood up, ignoring Miles's protestations. "Do not worry. I am taking a great many men with me. I rather hope they do try something on the road so that we can deal them the thrashing they deserve. Besides, you will need to take care of yourself here. If they know you, which is likely, you too could be in danger."

The thought had already crossed Miles's mind. It would make sense for them to keep a man or two in town to keep watch. Miles only hoped the scarred messenger was one of them.

The following day, with the permission of the Infirmarian, Miles was allowed to get up from his bed and walk around a little. Although the Infirmarian wanted to keep a close eye on his wounded shoulder, he knew that trying to keep a knight cooped up for days on end would only cause more trouble for him. Knights made very bad patients. However, his one condition was that he didn't go alone, but had to take Brother John with him, just in case exhaustion overwhelmed him.

Such fussing annoyed the knight. He didn't need a nursemaid, and he had no idea where John was. However, he didn't want to miss this opportunity. So, promising to go and find his friend, he went off on his own. It was only a small lie, but one the old monk didn't question.

Miles first took a stroll through the herb garden, which could be easily accessed from the infirmary. In the warm sunshine, the very air seemed full of life, except Miles's mind was concerned with quite the opposite. The death of his brother lay heavy on him indeed, and he would not rest until he had found the one responsible for Will's murder. In truth, that was his goal. Although he detested traitors, he would leave the matter of treason to be dealt with by the Baron de Witton. All he wanted was justice for Will, and he swore he would get.

He followed the path, leading out of the herb garden and into the open fields beyond. Brothers and lay brothers were hard at work. He turned away, and followed the path towards the Abbey's heart, and then, on seeing the gate open, decided to ignore the Infirmarian's advice and take a walk into town. He wouldn't catch a murderer stuck behind the abbey walls.

And yet, he hadn't taken more than two steps beyond the abbey when the familiar voice of Brother John called out to him, asking him to wait. It seemed that the Infirmarian hadn't believed Miles after all.

"Where are you going?" Brother John gasped, trying to get his breath back. The monk was not as fit as his friends, but then, he wasn't required to be. He had a different calling.

"For a walk."

"Should you be really going so far? You've been in bed for days."

"John, you can either come with me or go back inside," Miles said, patiently. "I don't mind which you do, as long as you stop nagging."

Brother John sighed and then indicated for his friend to lead the way. "I know you're up to something," he said, quietly, but Miles ignored him. "Well?" he pressed. Again he was met with silence.

Miles turned up the main thoroughfare and made his way towards the bridge, town, and castle. Crossing the bridge, he paused on the other side of the river, taking a good look around him.

"Now are you going to tell?" John asked, looking thoroughly bored and yet suspicious. He was not fond of the world outside of the abbey.

"If you were staying in the town for more than a few days but needed to keep an eye on the castle, where would you stay?"

John looked about him, considering the question for a moment. "In an inn or tavern close to the castle."

Miles smiled. He and John had both reasoned the same. "Let's go then."

John looked confused. "Go where? You haven't said where we are going?"

"The Seven Sisters, The Bear, The Star and The White Hart," Miles answered, reeling off all the taverns closest to the castle.

"But why?"

Miles set off in the direction of the first inn, describing the man they were looking for as they went. Now John understood what was going on, he was more inclined to help. They split up to go and make their enquiries.

However, when they met back up by the bridge a little while later, it was only to confirm that their search had borne no fruit. None recognised the description of the scar-faced man, and Miles rather dejectedly mused to himself there would be no mistaking him. If anyone had seen him, they would most certainly have remembered.

Miles had been certain that they were on the right track. Glumly he walked over to a few stalls lining the street, wondering what to do next. He didn't want to give up yet.

"Shall we try some of the taverns a littler further away from the castle?" Brother John asked, as Miles bought an apple from a stallholder whilst the monk, who was forbidden from eating outside of the abbey, gave the man a blessing.

"No. Any further away and there would be no point."

"What if he wasn't watching the castle but was inside it."

Miles nodded half-heartedly. "You could be on to something, but he wouldn't have been in the castle. His face was already known there."

"Could he have been watching the London road?"

"It's a possibility, but there are other roads out of the town. It would be a gamble to concentrate on just the one. I think you were closer with your first thought."

They continued on in silence for a while, the only sound to disrupt it was Miles eating his apple.

"How close can you get to the castle without getting inside it?" John asked whilst watching Miles throw his apple core into the ditch. "As you say, he would stand out too much within the walls, but lurking outside it, amongst the beggars that are often to be found there…perhaps there he would blend in more…"

Miles smiled, clapping his friend on the back. "Come, let us go find out."

With a step lightened with hope, Miles led the way towards the castle. His pace was eager now, his mood full of anticipation.

As they reached the market square, Miles felt a light touch on his arm. John was standing close but pulled him closer.

"Don't turn around, but I think I have just spotted our quarry."

Miles carried on looking straight ahead, pretending to still be about his business. "Where?" he asked tersely as he felt himself tense.

"Standing to your right, near the baker's stall."

The knight positioned himself slowly, trying to act as naturally as he could, but he needn't have bothered. When his eyes alighted on the man whose face was split in half by a bold scar and saw the smile that played across his face, a smile meant for him, Miles felt something in him give.

Seeing red, he set off after the man who had murdered his brother.

As Miles gave chase, his heart filled with revenge and murder. All thoughts of justice disappeared as he recalled what this animal had done to Will. He planned to get hold of him, make him reveal who else was involved and then dispatch him. No trial. No hanging.

The scarred man dashed up an alleyway. Miles was gaining on him. Although he had spent a few days confined to his bed, the messenger was not as fit as he was. Neither was he as young.

The passageway brought them up onto the street between castle and river. The chase had caught the attention of some of the guards at the gatehouse, some of whom were now following behind. Where Brother John was, the knight had no clue. Miles focused on the man in front of him, putting all distractions aside. His hand reached down to his belt and fingered his dagger, the only weapon he had thought to bring with him, but it would do. A man could die just as well on the end of a dagger as a sword, which was just as well as Miles's shoulder had not recovered enough to use the heavier, longer blade.

The man swerved around a group of men, sending one of them stumbling into the path of Miles.

"Move! Out of the way!" he called, desperately trying to not lose sight of his brother's murderer.

Quickly Miles realised that the messenger was heading straight for the river. On the steep bank, he paused for a second, turning to smile once more at his pursuer. He must have known about Miles's injury. They both knew that the injured knight couldn't swim the river well enough not to drown and to catch the man he was after.

Miles's ire rose as the man believed he was safe; he believed he was going to get away. His confident sneer made Miles push even harder, causing his lungs to feel like they were burning in his chest.

The distance was closing. Miles was almost upon him as the man turned away and jumped down the bank.

As Miles reached the edge, skidding to a halt, what he saw was unexpected. The guards from the castle who had joined in the pursuit, were quickly alongside him, looking down at the body of the messenger below them. His head was at an odd angle and resting upon on boulder at the water's edge. Blood was trickling down its sides and into the river.

One of the guards told the other to go and check if he was dead, as he turned to Miles and said, "Well, at least his stupidity saved you from committing murder."

A few days later, the Baron Hugh de Witton returned from London, laden with honours for bringing a matter of treason to the King's attention. He immediately called for Miles Chevalier, who arrived at the castle alongside Brother John. Together they told of the fate of the scarred messenger.

"He had obviously landed wrong as he jumped down the embankment, tripping and banging his head as he fell," Brother John concluded. "It was enough to kill him instantly."

"Just as well, I suppose," Hugh said, a wry smile playing upon his lips. "No doubt having one of my Knight's murder him on the riverbank would have looked very ill for us all indeed. Then the King might have changed his mind about endowing Will Chevalier's family, that is, you Miles, with the manor at Bromford."

Miles didn't know what to make of this gift he had been given. What would he do with his own manor? He had no need of it and the only reason he had it now was because Will was dead. He knew which he would rather have.

Goblets of wine were passed around and then raised in honour of Will. Justice had been done. The brother of Miles Chevalier could now rest in peace.

Licking Arrows

Shane Porteous

Ondame 12, that was the official name of the fort. A practical yet unimaginative name, but forts were supposed to be practical, and Ondame 12 wasn't the exception. It was a well-built fortress, one that had never fallen, of course, those two things were the same two things that could be said about any fort, until it fell.

Captain Neldalin was aware of this, just like he was aware there was a first time for everything and on this night he was more aware of this than he had ever been in his entire life. Because this was the first night that he was facing battle and felt afraid. The captain was neither a fool nor a braggart. But he was an experienced warrior, he knew what truly went on when battle commenced, he knew much more than the fact that spears, swords, and axes could kill people. He knew how they could be used to kill people and in much more detail than simply they were stuck through someone's skin and blood poured out.

Just like he knew there was far more to the enemy than a mere raiding party, he had fought against raiding parties before, had hunted them down to the last man or woman, had made raiders pay the price for pillaging the villages of the empire. Raiding parties didn't attack forts, forts were far too formidable to be taken by mere raiders, and yet seven of the twenty forts in Ondame had been crushed like stomped on sandcastles. He didn't need more convincing than that to know the enemy he would face on this night was something far more formidable than mere raiders, something far more formidable than even Ondame 12 and that is why he was afraid.

He knew there was always a chance of being killed in battle, someone who never even wielded a weapon knew that. But before this night there had always been a reasonable chance for victory, normally he could smell it in the stratosphere, the way a starving wolf tasted blood in the air, there was always a chance the wolf could find what was bleeding and fill its stomach. But Neldaline felt like a hungry wolf that couldn't smell anything.

Who the enemy exactly was he didn't know, but he knew who he was, and he knew who would stand by his side to defend this fort. Soldiers that had pissed someone off, soldiers or lower officers who had had the audacity to put their superiors in their place. Neldaline's great crime had been breaking the jaw of a superior officer who had tried to force himself onto a young boy. Neldaline didn't need his decade-plus experience in the Army to know you never touched a child that way. But what his decade more of military service did teach him was there were consequences to smacking superior officers in the face. His sentence had taken some time to commence, for the Colonel whose jaw was crushed wouldn't dare punish him, not in the boy's home city where whispers would spread, whispers that could lead to rations being withheld from soldiers the next time they sought refuge there.

But Ondame 12 was nowhere near that boy's city, and the villagers and workmen that once called this place home had their own whispers, whispers about what was coming to destroy this place. The same feeling he had felt when saving the boy from the Colonel was what filled him now, that he had done the right thing sending the villages and workmen into the woods away from Ondame 12. But just like then, he was aware of the potential consequences. There was a chance that some of them would whisper about how they had been sent away, that they had been forced to leave the protection of the fort. But it was hard to whisper with a slashed throat, and that is what would have happened to them if they stayed in the fort, just as Neldaline was sure his own throat would suffer said slicing. Many men and women were going to die tonight, Neldaline saw no point in adding to the body count. They didn't deserve to die and neither did he, but again he knew enough about death to know corpses didn't need company.

Apart from his fellow punished the only other people now in Ondame 12 were a handful of criminals crawling around the cells in the lower parts of the brickwork. There was a piece of him that wanted to free them as well, this was to be his punishment, not theirs. But there was always a chance that those in the cell had done far worse than punching a pedophile, chances were they were the kind of people that should've been punched. Then again if that was the worse thing that happened to them on this night than they should consider themselves lucky, something Neldaline was so far from feeling he almost couldn't fathom the meaning of the word.

As afraid as he was his steps didn't show it, they were strong, sturdy steps, over a decade of dancing across battlefields had trained his body never to tremble. He was moving through one of the walkways within the fort, one protected from the world beyond its bricks, a piece of him wanted to stay within it, a much larger piece of him made him keep moving. As he left the protected place into a more opened courtyard, a woman soldier came into his sight, marching with the same meticulousness as he did.

Before this night he had hadn't known her at all, now he knew enough of her to know her name was Korret, and her great crime had been not dancing with a general, no matter how loudly he demanded that she did so. The General hadn't listened to her when she explained how badly her feet felt after a full day of fighting and that she wouldn't be able to walk to the next battlefield without resting them. For a man who had worked his way up to command entire armies, the General didn't seem to understand how important the ability to walk was for a warrior. But every man and woman now in Ondame 12 knew why they had been sent there, to die defending a fort the colonels and generals of the empire weren't willing to fight for. No, the destruction of a dozen less desirable forts would only make their eventual involvement more triumphant. They would swoop in with a sizeable army, one large enough to challenge any kingdom, let alone whoever was raiding the forts.

His fellow punished had pondered over who exactly the raiders really were, and the most common guess was they were actually an advance party probing for weakness. They were looking for a good place to pull a piece of the empire away for themselves, like bears biting off a chunk of flesh from a wounded wilder beast. If that were the case, they would be no mere raiders, they would be professional soldiers, and ones trained specifically to slaughter forts like Ondame 12 and whomever they found inside them.

Even fools would think twice about attacking the empire, and the crushing of the forts would be foolish unless they could flee back to a formidable army, one capable of eroding large pieces of an empire.

They reached each other, both of their faces bearing the same mask of military misery.

"Is everyone in position?" Neldaline asked, his voice as dry and dull as a leaf in fall.

"Every soldier has been spread evenly…Captain," Korret replied, her voice accented by the same autumn.

Neldaline nodded, but there was no enthusiasm in such a gesture, just acceptance, like one who has suffered gangrene, accepts the amputation.

"Has everyone except us punished and the prisoners been cleared of the fort?"

"Not yet Captain," she answered, a small shift in her tone.

Neldaline narrowed his eyes, even though he was aware that tonight would probably be the last night of his life and the lives of the people he commanded, he still commanded them and thus he still expected them to fulfill their duties down to the letter.

Before he could speak, she did so, in a voice that wasn't as dry as it once had been.

"There are reports of a hooded woman in the third tower."

"The third tower?" Neldaline replied and for a moment, he seemed genuinely puzzled by the name. "You mean where we have stored all our extra arrows? Has someone investigated the claim?"

"Several soldiers have, or so they have claimed."

"And?" Neldaline asked, wondering if this was true then why wasn't the woman escorted away.

"The locals warned our fellow soldiers to stay away from her and not in the way a man warns another man to stay away from his wife. The way a man warns another man to stay out of the woods because of wolves, for their own benefit."

For a second it seemed like Neldaline's eyes and expression had sunken into his head.

"I'll investigate it," he said, the dryness replaced with frustration. "In the meantime, may you please double check that everyone is armed, ready and in position. The attack shall soon commence."

"That I will captain," Korret replied, her tone so dry that Neldaline actually felt thirsty hearing it.

They moved past each other without looking back as Neldaline marched across the courtyard, silently cursing. This was the last thing he needed. There was only one reason why the woman would be hooded on a hot night like this. Because she was a witch, or at least believed herself to be a witch the way Beragud of Blisskul, believed himself to be a bear on the nights when he had drunk far too much beer and found himself in the woods, roaring at the moon. Beragud did a pretty good imitation of such an animal, so much so that the occasional passerby often grasped their crossbows, fearing a bear was ready to bit them. That was of course until they saw the man himself, big-bellied and bearded, then they would let go of their crossbows and simply chuckle. But for those who never saw Beragud they still believed that there was a bear somewhere in the woods. By the same token, or so he imagined, many of the locals would consider this woman a witch, just like he was sure many of locals hadn't actually seen her. The problem was, and it was his problem now, was that if the woman were seen being dragged away by his fellow punished, the locals would spread whispers about the event, and no doubt the fort would be considered cursed, being the witch hadn't been allowed to wonder.

The last thing he needed was the locals running off to the enemy and feeding them information about the fort, punishing the already punished for having the audacity to get the woman out of harm's way. For even though the locals had been sent into the woods the captain was sure a few were still keeping eyes on the fort.

Plus, his fellow soldiers were desperate and desperate people were willing to believe things that were hard to believe. He could easily imagine them giving in to the woman, allowing her freedom, just in case she cursed them. They already had enough things against them this evening, they didn't need the wrath of a witch to worry about, real or otherwise. Common sense had been swept aside, because common sense said they were all going to die tonight, maybe if they believed the woman was actually a witch, that would somehow make the highly likely not so likely and somehow by leaving her alone they would survive.

Neldaline would have none of it though. The only thing he had left in this world was his position in the army, he was a captain and any captain that would allow a non-soldier free range of an armory, wasn't worthy of such a title. But he was worthy, he was as sure of that as he was of the reason why he had been sent here.

As he marched along the walkway he met the eye of every soldier he passed. They looked at him both with respect and the commonality they were going to become corpses before the night was over. Marching towards the third tower he stopped only once, when his eyes met the glazed over gaze of a woman soldier. She had only half-turned, her hand not on her weapon but holding something behind her waist. She said nothing when he stepped over, did nothing when he reached around and took what she was holding. He drank deeply from the jug, the wine washing through his system like rain upon a field. He handed it back to her and nodded, a gesture she returned as he patted her on the shoulder.

That was the thing about suicidal situations, it didn't matter if you were drunk or sober, the situations didn't change. It mattered not if his soldiers were drunk or sober, the enemy would still attack and it was probably something they wouldn't survive, at least they wouldn't have to worry about hangovers in the morning, dead people didn't have to worry about things like that.

He almost smiled at the thought.

Long before he had reached the third tower he could see that its door remained opened, anyone, whether ally or enemy could walk through it unchallenged. When he looked at the closest soldier to the entrance, there was a scolding look in his eyes, but when he saw just how scared the soldier was, he said nothing. His eyes looked to the man's waist, wanting to see if he had any wine to drink. But he didn't, the soldier grasped his spear firmly, even though the rest of him seemed on the brink of shaking. Neldaline couldn't blame him for being scared, even if he wanted to blame him for allowing the door to be opened. But he left it alone, giving himself the weak excuse that if he expected the woman to leave the tower the door had to stay open.

He entered the darkness without collecting one of the torches, the few within the tower itself burned brightly enough to guide his way as he walked up the winding steps. He saw shadows within the flames, but none of them moved, thus none of them frightened him. Still he found his hand upon his sword and not just to ensure its sheave didn't scrape against the steps. He could hear a faint sound from above, like a trickle of rainfall somewhere in the distance, he didn't know why but his hand then grasped his sword even tighter.

Reaching the final room of the tower, he was no longer in reach of firelight, but moonlight mauled enough of the room for him to see her, the hooded woman. Within that light he could see she was crouched, her back towards him, her garments as green as grass during spring. He also saw the arrows within her hand, held like a bundle of sticks being prepared for a fire. He watched on as seemingly she brought their tips into her mouth and then moved them away. The arrowheads shone within the moonlight, not just with steel but salvia. Confused, the captain did nothing but watch as the woman moved more arrows to her lips and licked their heads, before returning them to the piles from whence they came. It was only when she turned her head ever so slightly, that Neldaline was taken out of his trance. He couldn't see her face yet, but he could see enough to view her tongue tunneling into the air and licking the arrows in her hand before she calmly put them back in place. The captain had every reason to be confused, in all the ways he had seen people use arrows, this had been the first time he had seen someone licking them like lollipops.

She might not have been an actual witch, just like Beragud wasn't an actual bear, but that didn't mean that

Beragud couldn't be dangerous, he was strong enough to break your neck, he didn't need claws to rip out your throat. He didn't know how this woman could kill, but he was now certain she was capable of it and thus his hand was ready to rip out the sword from his sheave. She stood up with the kind of calm a spider does after it has sunk its fangs into a fly, a creepy kind of calm. But when she turned and he saw her face, both of his hands moved, away from any weapon, opened palmed above his shoulders, the universal sign of surrender.

Her eyes weren't quite yellow, they were more the shade of beach sand, but they were close enough to that colour for him to know what kind of creature she was, hence why he had raised his hands. She was of a breed that belonged within a certain woods, where the leaves were a dark red all year round. Where true witches and real shape-shifters were born. He studied her face the way one studies the sharp teeth of a lioness right before she lunges upon you and tears your throat out. He could see her teeth, even though she was neither smiling nor snarling, they looked like fishhooks, filling her mouth. Her hair was as black as burnt sticks, lavish long locks that looked like thin leeches lurking down from her scalp. They framed her face the way the night frames a star.

"Captain Neldaline," she said and he didn't know whether to be frightened or flattered that she knew his name.

Her voice was as morbid as music played during a midnight massacre. A voice that wasn't so much dark as a voice that told darkness what to do.

"My lady," he said, in a tone that was anything but dry.

In that moment, he forgot about the pedophile he had punched, of Korret, of the raiders that had destroyed seven forts and were eager to add an eighth. All he thought about was where this woman had come from and how creatures from those woods had to be treated.

"It isn't safe here, for your own well-being I plead with you to get as far away from this fort as you can."

The woman watched him the way he was sure a bear watched a rabbit and not a bear like Beragud, but a real ravenous bear.

"I am aware of that Captain," she said without arrogance.

Neldaline didn't notice his own hands as they lowered and his eyes narrowed.

"Have you? Have you?" he repeated. "Have you come to fight alongside us?" he asked with the curiosity of a child.

The empire he served was powerful, but there was nothing more powerful than the woods where this woman came from.

"I have come to ask you for a favor," she said. "There is a bootlegger being held prisoner here, a young man called Kuros, I would like you to pardon him of his crime."

Neldaline clenched his teeth, but kept his lips lucid. He was fully aware of the temporary power he had over the fort, he could certainly grant this bootlegger what she had asked. Just like he was fully aware that she could certainly help his cause, if she was so inclined. But seemingly she wasn't interested in that, for all their power and prestige those who called those woods home were a selfish species. Caring only for what the gods had bestowed on them, nothing else mattered. Certainly not the lives of the men and women who didn't deserve to die here.

"My lady…" he began, his words drifting off like dust in the wind.

"Sanel," she said, causing him further pause.

She had misunderstood him, he hadn't expected her name, rather he was contemplating whether it was worth cursing this woman out, he was going to die here anyway, what punishment could she lay upon him?

He was willing to find out, that was before she spoke again.

"Captain? From what I have heard you are a fair man."

He said nothing in response, now wondering what this woman had heard.

"Would you consider it fair if I fight for this fort tonight? Fought well enough that not only you survived, but the fort remained standing, in exchange for a pardon for Kuros?"

A troop of thoughts marched through his mind, mostly uniformed in the same questions, why would she be willing to do that? And just who was this Kuros? His mouth moved as if to speak, but then a sound screamed into the air.

The hum of a battle horn.

His head turned sharply, while her head didn't turn at all towards the sound. The enemy was about to make their first move.

"Captain?" Sanel said, her voice strong enough to make him look back at her. "Do you consider that fair?"

He could hear murmurs of marching, both from enemy and ally alike, outside of the tower.

"Yes," he said. "Protect this fort and I will pardon this Kuros."

She gave a single nod before moving towards the window. It was tall enough for her to stand in without slumping. She stood strong, the moonlight moving around her, making her appear both magnificent and monstrous, like the only wolf in a world of weaklings. She didn't leap so much as lean off the edge, falling towards the ground below. More startling than her actions were the actions of the arrows, they leapt up from the piles, following her in her flight like moths following torchlight. It all happened fast enough for the captain to move towards the window and witness as she landed below. Her knees did not even buckle as the arrows landed in well-organized lines on either side of her, becoming two neatly stacked piles. The sound of them assembling was like cards being shuffled by a master poker player, when they were finished not a single arrow was out of place.

Neither was she, it was as if as soon as Sanel had landed the courtyard belonged to her. It was a small courtyard, but it was more valuable than any of the other courtyards. Not just because it was the one she was in, but because the captain knew this is where the enemy would begin their attack, which is why he had chosen the third tower to keep the arrows in. He hoped they would be swarming over the walls and into this courtyard where his fellow punished could pepper them with arrows, the smaller the space the harder it would be for them to maneuver out of harm's way. It was an old tactic, but a great tactic nevertheless. Just because enemy victory had been all been assured, didn't mean Neldaline and his fellow punished were going to make it an easy victory.

He had no idea what she was going to do with the arrows, but he had a feeling they were more valuable next to her than they would have been within the armory. He became transfixed by her, watching and waiting to see what she was going to do.

That was of course before a shadow moved within the moonlight, one large enough to block out most of the moon. He looked up and saw it, a boulder as big as a storm cloud, moving through the air, towards the tower. He had been right, the attackers weren't a mere raiding party, no raiding party possessed a catapult.

"Brace!" he called out below, his voice carried through the fort, it was the only thing he could do, none of the punished had been prepared for a catapult. He watched as it sailed towards the tower, quickly dropping to his knees in preparation. That is when the boulder became lit, as if it was an ember fleeing a giant fire, it then exploded so violently that not so much as a single pebble struck the tower. The dust it had been destroyed into was so fine that it was actually carried off by the wind. He didn't have to look around to any of the walkways to know his fellow punished also had their heads raised, pondering what had happened to the projectile.

That is when more boulders came, proving the attacking force was far better equipped than the defending force. Yet each boulder suffered the same fate as the first, glowing like an ember and then exploding into dust. The punished watched on as before long the exploding boulders began to look like fireworks. In his decade-plus of dealing with death Neldaline had never seen anything quite like it before, he doubted anyone within Ondame 12 had, except…

He found his gaze lowering to the green garment wearing Sanel. Unlike the punished that had gotten on their knees or at least ducked their heads she stayed still as if fully aware the boulders couldn't bring any harm to the fort. Before he could wonder if the boulders were some form of magical pollution he saw something move away from her, something that he could only see because she was standing in the moonlight. Little lines of black were fleeing her hood and rising into the air, each one touching a boulder, before each boulder became an ember and exploded. He had seen her licking arrows, but that didn't make the sight easier to accept. Strands of her hair were leaving her scalp and somehow causing the boulders to explode. He was so mesmerized by it that his eyes no longer raised to see the boulders blow up. That was of course until the boulders no longer blew up.

His eyes shifted from her to the wall, back and forth. It appeared the enemy had run out of ammo, without a single causality caused.

"Stay ready!" he called out, hearing his words echoed by all punished within earshot, ensuring all those who weren't had heard his command.

The night had become quiet again, no doubt the enemy weighing their options, whatever they chose he hoped they would be in reach of Sanel's hair. He then heard a scraping sound as did those on the closest walls, as did everyone in the city. Before he could hazard a guess as to what it was, the wall from where the boulders had been flung over was cut in twain. He now stood fully, his knees forgetting entirely how to bend.

Unable to fathom what he was seeing, within the moonlight he could see it, something that shone like steel and looked like the top of a sword, if said sword was the size of a steeple. But then he became even more bewildered, for the sword seemed to be growing teeth, metal teeth, but teeth none the less. The teeth bit down on either severed side of the wall, holding on like a tiger biting into a bull's back. A second passed and the giant blade was pulled back, bringing the two sides with it, as if dragging its kill off into the darkness. Within seconds the wall had been completely removed from the fort and to top it all off, it was a completely clean cut as if the fort was always meant not to have wall there. This wasn't a raiding party, nor was it an ordinary enemy army, at least none he had ever heard of before and Neldaline had heard of hundreds of different kinds.

From the darkness they came, dozens at first, soon followed by hundreds pouring in like angry ants out of a nest. They seemed like warriors from another world, because they possessed armor unlike any the captain had ever seen, blue and beetle-like, as if these soldiers had skinned giant bugs to build their cuirasses. They each wielded a spear or sword, but they all had shields, inscribed with an insignia no country he knew of claimed.

It took the sight of an arrow being buried into one of their necks for him to realize where he was again. He looked across the walkways and saw several soldiers firing arrows into the oncoming horde.

"Fire at will!" he called out, ensuring the few archers that were just standing still, were doing so no longer.

Knowing it was best to lead by example, he took the bow from his back and plucked an arrow upon it, though he did not fire, frozen by the sight of just how many there were. No wonder seven forts had already fallen; it would take a considerable army to withstand them.

That or many well-aimed arrows.

He glanced to either side of the room, noticing how few arrows remained there. That is when he looked back down at Sanel and all the arrows at her sides. She still hadn't moved, even though the entire enemy force was madly marching towards her. It made a terrible sense, she was the only defender not standing on a wall, the only defender they could reach with ease. That is when it happened, the arrows left the ground one after the after, like soldiers assembling in the air to form an army, an army that rushed straight into the enemy line. The arrow remained fully stretched on his bow, he didn't have to strain to keep it there, because his whole body felt frozen, marveling at the massacre that was taking place below him. Each arrow didn't just cut through one enemy soldier, but many, bouncing around with such swiftness that enemy soldiers were lifted into the air as the arrows assaulted them repeatedly. Sanel walked forward, the arrows moving in all directions, destroying everything in the court, but maintaining a circle of safety around her where they would not fly. Within the moonlight the arrows looked black, like they were ravens, tearing apart the enemy soldiers, creating breadcrumbs out of them. Even the sound the arrows made was like the flapping of dark wings, the screams of the enemy sounding like squawks. Neldaline didn't need to tell any of his soldiers to stop firing, they did so on their own, watching as Sanel walked forward looking like she was walking through a snowstorm of blood, bodies and black arrows.

The arrows didn't stop their apocalypse until they themselves were annihilated, their shafts shattered, their tips torn apart by wear and tear. The crumbs of the corpses that had been in the air all came down at once, revealing that there wasn't a single body that remained intact amongst the enemy. Sanel stopped dead in the center of the courtyard where still a perfect circle of safety remained around her, even though the arrows had long since been destroyed.

The only answer to the annihilation Neldaline could come up with was this had been the reason why Sanel had been licking arrows. In any case he certainly was correct in feeling that they were more valuable with her than within the tower.

But now the only thing he could think of was why had Sanel stopped, remembering that she had a better view of what lay beyond the sliced apart wall. His eyes moved from her just as things began to appear from the black, a cruel coincidence indeed. These weren't men armored to look like bugs, these weren't men at all, or women, or human. There were ten of them strolling from the darkness like bears out of caves. They possessed long flowing hair, like women, but there was nothing human about them. Their bodies were a light black, designed to move on all fours, with tails like whips and faces like demons. Their eyes glowed a mixture of orange and blue, changing between the two colours like some kind of kaleidoscope. Though they were far fewer in number they were far more frightening than the hundreds that had come before, not least of which was the fact Sanel was out of arrows.

They charged into the courtyard like hunting dogs hungry for a hare. No one fired a single arrow, because the beasts were so bewildering. Neldaline had fought against many kinds of men, but had never seen beasts like these, let alone fought them. He hoped then and there that the same couldn't be said about Sanel, considering she was the first thing they would reach and rip apart.

Calmly, the word couldn't be more stressed, Sanel raised her hands before her, her fingers and thumbs as straight as arrows, before the digits disengaged off of her hands bloodlessly. The 8 fingers and two thumbs moved through the air with the precision of crossbow bolts, each one finding the neck of a beast, barreling into them like worms into soil. The fingers and thumbs purged through the flesh, each one completing a full rotation of their necks, separating their heads from their shoulders. It had been done so quickly that none of the beasts snarled or stopped, they kept moving, although they all bled, their severed bodies slipping in their own blood and becoming still amongst all the other corpses. Before their heads had struck the ground, Sanel's fingers and thumbs were already back upon her hands, each wriggling for a moment as if happy to be home, or happy about they harmed they caused, or both. But soon they became still once again and that could mean only one thing.

Captain Neldaline, who only now realized he still had an arrow stretched and plucked on his bow, looked back into the darkness beyond the wall, imagining what new kind of monster was about to march into the courtyard. The ground then began to shake, followed by the third tower and then the whole fort shook, as if frightened. His arm relaxed and the bowstring was no longer stretched, he felt no relief in his arm because of this, considering he had a feeling, now more than ever, that he would need to use this weapon, very, very soon.

It was hard to tell if it moved out of the darkness or if the darkness moved out of its way. The latter wouldn't surprise Neldaline, considering the chill this thing sent through his body was so severe; he looked down at his chest genuinely expecting to see cuts. He looked back upon the behemoth, a being so big that the tip of the tallest trees would scratch its chin. It was a dark shade of purple, save for the red sword sized spikes that mohawked its head. It had a face that was familiar, so much as it had two eyes, one nose and one mouth, but it didn't possess a feature that wasn't freakish, a feature that wasn't frightening. Its body bulged with muscle, even its smallest thew was the size of a table top. Its sheer size and strength would've allowed it to throw boulders like they were pebbles. It seemed the enemy didn't have catapults at all, although that brought Neldaline absolutely no comfort. Because the giant wielded a blade that matched its size. The same blade that had sliced and then bit into the wall, removing it out of the giant's path. The sword didn't shine so much in the moonlight as it reveled in it, revealing the monstrous face within the metal, it was so ghastly it was hard to tell who possessed the fiercest face, the blade or the behemoth. Both faces bore expressions of anger as both seemed to be searching the courtyard, as if the sword was as much a living breathing thing as the beast that wielded it.

It was so close to the fort now that the shakes it summoned took Neldaline off of his feet, along with every other punished within Ondame 12. This time he willingly stayed close to the ground, lifting himself up just enough to peer back into the courtyard. The giant didn't have to look long, it approached Sanel with sinister steps, but no matter how much it made the ground shake, the green garment-wearing woman remained still. The only movement she made was the slight tilting of her head, so she could see into its angry accusing eyes. It didn't blink and although Captain Neldaline couldn't see her eyes, he was sure Sanel didn't blink either, not even when the giant raised its sword and the face upon the blade bared its metal teeth as if silently snarling.

The shadow of the blade completely blocked out the moonlight, leaving the world in the most dangerous kind of darkness. Captain Neldaline did the only thing he could, "Sanel!" he screamed, not knowing how that would help, but he couldn't just stand by and watch her get sliced in half.

The blade descended, but not very far, just enough to allow a little moonlight to reach the courtyard. The illumination was intense and still the captain was bewildered by what he saw. The first thing he noticed was the sword hadn't gotten very far, it remained in the air, far above Sanel. The second thing he noticed was just how freaked out the frightening face within the metal now looked, like a man who woke up to find a snake biting upon his belly. The third thing was what had actually stopped the blade. It looked almost like a vine, hanging perfectly still off the sword, but it was red and fleshy.

When Neldaline realized what it was, he forgot how to count.

Sanel's tongue had moved from her mouth, growing at least 14 feet up in the air and stopping the blade with its tip. Neldaline stared at the contact point between the tongue and the blade, expecting to see blood. It was one thing to think she had stopped the blade with her tongue, it was quite another to believe she had done so without blood loss. Yet he couldn't see blood, but he could see something that shone in the moonlight, the same thing that had once made the arrows shine within the third tower. Her salvia was soaking the sword, causing the face upon it to look like it was cursing. Then the metal face went from terrifying to terrified and silently it began to scream.

The face of the monster didn't change, in expression at least, although it was cut in half, cleaner than the wall had been. The sword had suddenly went backwards slicing through the monster from scalp to scrotum, tearing through it like a knife through a tomato. The blood that began to flow from the cut certainly looked like vegetable juice. Its death had been that swift that its hand still kept a grasp upon the giant sword even as the two halves fell to the ground, causing the fort to shake one more time.

A garrison of gasps marched into the air as every soldier who saw it, made such a sound, beginning with Neldaline, he was a good commander after all, he was still leading by example. The gasps then became ghosts as Sanel's tongue moved in the air, not retracting back into her mouth, at least not yet. The tongue whipped near the ground, moving over an arrow, one fired by a soldier and not her salvia, hence why it was still intact. The arrow moved out of the body and as her tongue retracted back into her mouth the arrow flew up through the tower window, just over Neldaline's head. He could feel the wind whisper through his hair, it told him to look at the far wall, where the arrow had struck, but not before it had claimed a piece of parchment and a wet quill, pinning both to the brickwork.

Neldaline didn't even know there was parchment or quills in the tower, but he knew what he had to do. Just like he knew he had to do it before Sanel reached him. He stood up and hurried over to the arrow, releasing it from the wall and taking quill and parchment in hand. He began writing the pardon before he could remember the prisoner's name.

Another garrison of gasps filled the air, prompting him to turn his head back to the world outside, but it was blocked by Sanel, who know stood within the window. He had no idea how she got back up there so quickly, but knew it was the reason why his fellow soldiers had gasped. Her tongue was back behind her teeth, although those fishhooks were horrifying enough on their own.

"I have fought, the enemy is dead, the fort still stands and you are still alive, that is fair," she stated more than asked. He felt his hand moving the quill before he realized he had written down the prisoner's name.

"That is fair," he said, signing the parchment before handing it to her.

Although she took it from him delicately, he was still weary of their fingers touching, not knowing the terror that would be unleashed on him if that were to happen. She moved back into the moonlight, allowing its luminosity to lurk over the page.

"My lady," he said both carefully and courteously.

Her eyes shifted from the parchment to meet his, the act somehow monstrous.

"That thing out there, the giant with the sword, that was an Arigaga Gorec wasn't it?"

To this she nodded, her focus already back upon the paper.

His teeth found his lip, wanting to chew right through it. He was angry, not at Sanel, but at the realization of why the generals and colonels had really wanted nothing to do with these forts. Because they knew the enemy wasn't an invading force, it was a monster, who led other monsters, a being so feared it was the very reason why a certain god had created beings like this Sanel to put an end to their miserable monstrous lives. A being so ferocious that the generals and colonels would never dare face it, even with a million men.

"I thought they were extinct," he spat.

According to the stories he had heard as a child they were supposed to be.

"So did I," said Sanel, in between reading the pardon. "Until tonight."

While Neldaline was angry she was almost apathetic about it, she had killed the Arigaga Gorec and its followers like they were nothing more than flies. She looked up from the pardon before folding it and placing it in her pocket.

"Thank you for keeping your end of the agreement, captain."

"Thank you for keeping yours," Neldaline replied, wondering if he had ever said anything more genuine in his whole life.

"Well, I shall collect Kuros and be on my way," Sanel said turning back towards the window.

But she had only gotten two steps when Neldaline said, "May I ask?" He waited for her to turn around. "What did this bootlegger do to get on your good side?"

She smiled, strangely even with her sharp teeth and dark eyes, her smile was far more motherly than monstrous.

"He had the luck of being a friend of a friend of mine."

"Well then," he said with a small smile of his own. "After I have gotten the sappers to fix the fort wall, I will return home and ask any of my friends if they know you."

To this, she merely stared but kept her motherly smile.

"At the moment I feel like being a bootlegger would be better than being a soldier," Neldaline then wondered how many of his fellow punished would agree?

Our Doubts Are Traders
Michelle Monagin

"Our doubts are traitors, and make us lose the good we oft might win, by fearing to attempt." - (Measure for Measure, Act I, Scene IV) – William Shakespear

The morning sun shone weakly through the slit of a window in the sitting room they had been given in her uncle's castle. From that window, Gwenaelle could see a square of light blue sky spotted with white clouds and the suggestion of green on the lower portion. Nothing more.

She wanted to see the tournament grounds with the flags of all the knights posted around it. She wanted to see the merchant stalls that were undoubtedly set up all around the grounds. She wanted to see all the people walking around, enjoying themselves during this weeklong holiday that the Duke had decreed. And, most of all these things, she wanted to see the zither the Duchess had ordered to be made as a prize to the finest troubadour at the tournament. She'd never seen a zither before.

Gwenaelle pulled away from the window with a sigh, sat down on a nearby bench seat and looked around at the sitting room disconsolately. The cushions and tapestries in this room were almost—not quite, but almost—threadbare. She could see places where the threads on the tapestries had broken and been fixed with threads of a slightly different color. The cushions were worse, with the pile of the ancient fabric obviously worn away in some places.

Her mother, Oanez, had not said anything about the state of the furnishings when they had arrived last night, and Gwenaelle had not had the courage to ask. She was afraid that they had been given this room as a sort of subtle insult to her father. But, maybe not. She knew so little of her father's status here. *Judoc would know,* she thought. Her brother had been sent as squire to her father's people, while she had gone to her grandmother's people on the coast.

Oanez came into the sitting room with her work-basket in her hands, and Gwenaelle had to work hard not to sigh again. *Why do I always have to sit inside sewing while things are happening outside,* she thought very quietly in a private part of her own mind.

Oanez's smile suggested that she knew exactly what Gwenaelle was thinking just then. Gwenaelle felt her face grow warm in a blush under her mother's knowing look, even though she was sure she had kept her thoughts in the private part of her mind. She sat up straighter and tried not to think again of the beautiful June morning outside the window.

Oanez sat down on the other end of the bench without a word. She placed the work-basket between them, bringing out the kirtle she was decorating with fine needlework. She sat for a moment, looking over the stitching she had done so far.

Gwenaelle could feel Oanez's concentration build before she even took up her needle. She couldn't tell what sort of spell her mother was weaving into the kirtle with her sewing, but she could feel the spell building as the flower design took shape. She had been too embarrassed to ask when she had first realized what Oanez was doing.

Protection? Maybe, but there was something else there, too. There was a subtle drawing of attention, not to the stitches themselves or to the kirtle, exactly. It was something new, something she had never seen in her mother's work. Gwenaelle thought it might draw the attention to her face. She found herself hoping her own feeble attempt would not clash with it.

Gwenaelle reached into the basket and brought out the pair of gloves she was embellishing with a complimentary design to the one her mother was sewing onto the kirtle, visually. She concentrated on the spell she was working into the gloves, trying to see if that would complement or clash with the spell her mother was sewing into the kirtle.

She decided that her own spell would complement what her mother was sewing afterall. She was trying to add grace to the gloves. She was hoping that, when she wore the gloves, she wouldn't drop things and draw negative attention. Whatever it was that her mother was sewing into the kirtle was similar, although it was more complicated.

Gwenaelle looked again at the kirtle in Oanez's hands. Her own work was not nearly so neat as her mother's. Neither the sewing nor the spell work. She wondered if it was just practice, or if there was something else. *Would I ever be able to sew such a spell into my own or another's clothing?*

"You sew so beautifully, Mother," she said, on the breath of another sigh. She could see her mother's dimple as she spoke.

"You do not sew too badly, my dear," her mother said, her eyes dancing. "You would do much better could you curb your impatience."

"I do try, sometimes," Gwenaelle said, and Oanez laughed. She smiled then. She never could resist her mother's laugh. It was deep and rich; it seemed to come right from the middle of her being, from her heart.

While they were talking and sewing, there came a knock at the outer door. The maid, Mari, came out of Gwenaelle's bedroom to answer it. Gwenaelle looked up to see who had come, her hands pausing in their sewing. Oanez kept her eyes down and continued with her work. Mari stepped away from the door to let someone come in.

Gwenaelle gave a cry of joy when she saw that it was her brother, Judoc. She jumped up, not noticing that her gloves fell to the floor when she did, and ran to embrace him. Judoc laughed and picked Gwenaelle up and twirled around with her in his arms. Gwenaelle laughed, too. She remembered when they were around the same size. Now Judoc towered over her and picked her up with no difficulty. No one would know that they were twins, now.

"It is well there is no one else here to see you two behaving so," Oanez's voice came from behind Gwenaelle, sounding both amused and disapproving.

Judoc's laugh came again, filling the small room, as he released his sister. "Come, mother," he responded. "Is it so strange that I am happy to see my second half?"

"T'would be as well," Roparzh's voice came from the doorway to their parents' bedroom behind them, and Judoc turned to include him in the conversation. "Not to refer to your sister in that way."

Gwenaelle noticed that her father was looking serious as he spoke and that he glanced at his wife. Gwenaelle looked back and forth between them, not understanding them or why Judoc's face had suddenly become serious as well. She was going to ask when her brother spoke.

"I am sorry, Father," Judoc said. "I spoke without thought. I will not let it happen again."

Roparzh nodded and smiled tightly at Judoc. "You look well, Judoc," he said. "I would swear that you have grown two hands since I saw you last."

"But he looks half starved," Oanez broke in. "Do they never feed you? Do they expect you to train without fuel?" She came and gave him a hug with a smile.

Judoc hugged their mother back, then turned and gave his hand to their father. "I am well, father," he said, smiling again. "I am glad you have come." He shared his smile between the three of them. "I am come this morning to take Gwenaelle on a tour of the fields if I may."

"Oh!" Gwenaelle exclaimed. "Oh, may I, Father?"

Roparzh was looking doubtfully at Gwenaelle. "We were going to the Duke's court this morning, and I wanted you there," he said. "I understand that the King of France is coming to the tournament. He's due in today."

"He won't be here until late this afternoon," Judoc told him. "Sir Alberic had word that the king's party spent the night at Vitre, and that they started late—long after the sun rose."

"Please, Father, Mother," Gwenaelle begged. "I have not seen Judoc for two years. Surely we can have a few hours to talk."

Roparzh still hesitated, but Oanez said, "You must take Mari." She was still smiling, but Gwenaelle could see that she would not move on this requirement. "You must have a chaperone at all times while we are in Rennes."

"But I don't have..." Gwenaelle started, but her father interrupted her.

"Rennes is not your home," he said. "You must do as we say while we are here."

Gwenaelle did not understand why she could not go about by herself here when she was accustomed to doing it at home and at Carnac, where she had been studying recently. But she decided not to argue. She seldom had seen her father look so serious as he had done since he decided to bring them along to the tournament, although he had not told her what it was that he was so unhappy about.

For the moment, she was willing to let that go, so long as she was allowed to spend some time with her twin brother. She agreed to take Mari.

Judoc talked easily as he steered Gwenaelle out of the castle and down to the tournament grounds to the northeast of the castle. Mari walked a little behind them, as befitted a servant, and said nothing. Gwenaelle found that it was easy to forget her presence as she listened to her brother's news.

Judoc spoke of the knight who had taken him on as a squire, Sir Alberic; of the other young men who were training alongside him; and a little bit about his training. He said nothing of any problems he might have encountered. Nor did he speak of their cousins.

Gwenaelle followed his lead until they had left the castle, before they reached the tournament grounds. When there was no one close enough to hear what she said except Judoc, she asked him about their cousins. He took a few moments before he answered her, looking at her out of the corners of his eyes.

"William and Louis," Judoc said, giving the boys the French equivalent of their names. "Are not interested in admitting the connection."

Gwenaelle was surprised at this. "But how can they deny there is a connection between us?" she asked. "Grandfather recognized father. I know that does not make him a legitimate son, and he can't inherit the castle here, even though he is older than Duke Alan. But it is well known that Father is Duke Alan's brother, is it not?"

"Yes, it is well known," Judoc replied, smiling. "And Father has always given good service—both to Grandfather and to Alan—so Alan does not despise the connection. But his sons have become enamored with the French court." He paused as they came abreast of two men walking the opposite way, toward the castle. He went on after they had gone past. "Did you know that they were squired to the French king?"

"No, I didn't know that," Gwenaelle answered slowly. "Although I suppose it doesn't surprise me."

"No. It is natural enough," Judoc said. He sighed. "Duke Alan had to send his boys off to train with someone else. It isn't done to train your own children—for lots of reasons. And the King of France has status enough to please anyone. But I wish he had chosen somewhere else to send them."

"Is that why you called them by the French equivalents of their names?"

"Oh, yes, they've become more French than the French," Judoc smiled down at Gwenaelle. "Their father is less than pleased. William came back a fortnight ago, newly made a knight, and there has been no end of argument. He thinks he doesn't have to follow his father's rules, now that he's Sir William." He paused. "Duke Alan calls him Sir Gwilherm." Judoc laughed shortly, cutting it short as they reached the tournament grounds.

They barely knew their two cousins, who were four and two years older than them, respectively. At least, Gwenaelle barely knew them. It sounded like Judoc knew them better than he cared to.

Gwenaelle was troubled by this evidence of conflict in her family, but she decided to keep it to herself until they were again alone. From the way Judoc acted, it wasn't generally known that Duke Alan was at odds with either of his sons. Instead of asking about it, she listened to his description of what would take place on these fields starting in the morning.

The first field they came to was a large area cordoned off by ropes with nothing inside it except grass and dirt. At the other side of this enclosure was a raised platform with seats and a roof. Judoc told her that was where Duke Alan and the French King and anyone either of them invited would sit to watch the melee. He explained that the melee was where two opposing 'armies'—actually small groups of knights—would fight each other.

"The point of this is not to kill," he assured her. "Although they do not use blunted weapons, so it is possible."

"And will you be in the melee?" she asked, frightened but trying not to show it to him.

Judoc shook his head. "Not I," he said, a little bit of pride leaking out of him, although he had managed to keep his tone off-hand. "I'll be jousting."

"But I thought only knights could joust?" Gwenaelle asked, surprised. Judoc was just seventeen years old—same as she was—and she had thought a man had to be at least nineteen to be considered for the accolade.

"I have been knighted," he said. He reached down and hugged her, and she could feel the excitement rolling off him in waves. "Last week. It's because of Sir Alberic. I went along the last time he patrolled the northern coast—well, I've gone along several times, since he's my patron. But this last time, we caught a troupe of rogues who had been preying on travelers to St. Malo. I did my share."

Gwenaelle did not ask many questions. She could feel the pride, but also something else. She suspected that he would not want to describe exactly what he had done, what his share was. She felt just a bit of what he was feeling—he was not embarrassed, exactly, or ashamed of what he had done, but he seemed to feel that it wasn't something a lady should be exposed to.

It felt odd to her that he was thinking of her as a lady, and even odder to think of the ways she and her twin brother seemed to be growing apart. She swallowed that thought. It was natural and right that Judoc should grow apart, become himself completely. At that moment, she was glad that he did not seem to be able to tell what she was thinking.

She smiled up at him proudly and said, "What more could we expect of my brother?"

They both laughed as they went on toward the merchant city that was set up on the other side of the tournament grounds. Gwenaelle had told Judoc about the zither that was a prize in the other competition this week, and he wanted to see it, too.

"I think Katarin wants to employ a troubadour here," Judoc told her. "At least, that is what Duke Alan told father."

"Oh, yes?" Gwenaelle asked somewhat absently. She was looking for a certain woodworker's stall. "That would be a very good thing for the duchy, if they can attract a good one."

"Hmm," Judoc said, smiling and looking at her out of the corner of his eyes. "And are you going to compete?"

Gwenaelle felt herself blushing. Judoc didn't seem to need any powers to be able to know what she was thinking, sometimes.

"I would like to compete," she admitted to Judoc, quietly, so that even Mari wouldn't hear. "I'm not sure, though."

"What are you not sure of?" asked Judoc, half-joking and half-serious. "That you would win? Or if you should compete?"

Gwenaelle shook her head in annoyance. "Competition is a way of finding out how good you are," she told him. "I don't know that I'd win, but I'd be willing to take the risk." She paused and looked up at him, wondering if he understood what she was saying. "I've been competing, at Carnac, for over a year."

He looked back at her in surprise, but he didn't respond, so she went on, "I'm just not sure how Father would react. He's been a little strange since we came to Rennes."

She felt a little nervous. Would Judoc think she was criticizing their father? But she had been hoping to speak to him about this very thing. She did not understand what was happening and she wanted to. How did they think she could support them if she didn't know what was going on?

Judoc nodded in understanding, his expression all serious now. "It is status," he said. "His status doesn't matter at home because he has it and everyone there admits it. He can let Grandmother follow the old ways, and even teach you the old ways, as long as he is at home. But here," Judoc gestured around at the fair and the castle. "Here, he is just one of the old duke's bastards."

"And the people here look down on the old ways," Gwenaelle didn't make this a question—she already knew the answer. "And on bastards?"

Judoc shrugged. "Most of them don't know anything about the old ways. Even the Duke knows little, and the duchess knows less." He paused, thinking, as if he were trying to say something he didn't quite know the shape of. "As to the question of bastardy… It's not really that. It's that Father spends so much time on his own estates. He hasn't been able to make friends, here." He grimaced. "Or allies."

"So I couldn't compete, then?" this was a question. "Because women don't compete, and Father doesn't want us to do anything different?"

"Now, that's not true," Judoc said. "There are women troubadours. Not many, it's true. But one of them has come to compete this week. And who could blame her, when she's competing for that."

They had reached the woodworker's stall, and Judoc nodded to the instrument that was on display, hanging on the pole just outside the tent. Gwenaelle caught her breath in a swallowed cry. She let go of his arm and went toward the tent like someone in a trance.

"It's glorious," she sighed.

It was unlike any instrument she had ever seen before. The fret was incorporated on one side of the zither, not coming out the top on a neck like her lute. There were five strings over the fret—those would be for playing the melody. There were twelve other strings next to the fret but not over it. Then there were seven other strings, secured at the bottom of the instrument as well as the others, but running up at an oblique angle to the first nineteen strings and fastened to a kind of neck to the other side. She itched to take it down and try to play it, to see what all the strings sounded like.

It was beautifully made, too. Obviously, it was crafted by a master craftsman. The body looked like satin in a reddish brown color. There was a ring around the sound hole in the body that was made of different types of wood—

lighter than the body—in a pattern that was echoed on the curved side of the zither. At the top was another type of wood, this one darker than the body.

Gwenaelle only realized how long she had been staring at the instrument when she heard someone speak behind her and her brother answer. She turned, her cheeks burning, to see the craftsman himself talking to Judoc.

"I'm sure she would like to try it," Judoc was saying. He smiled at her, and she stayed silent, letting him do the talking. "She's very good on a lute."

"Well, a zither is not exactly like a lute," the craftsman said. He looked at Gwenaelle, too, but he didn't smile. She imagined he thought she would unlikely to be able to play it.

"It's beautiful," she said, gesturing at the instrument before her. "How are these nineteen strings tuned? Are they fifths?" She saw the beginnings of a smile returned to her.

"Yes, they are called 'drone strings.' They are to give a background to the melody, which one plays on these five strings." The man looked around at the crowds passing by, then he asked, "Would you like to try it?"

Gwenaelle agreed eagerly, and the man brought a stool for her to sit on. He placed the zither in her lap and stepped back to watch. Gwenaelle ran a few scales to make herself familiar with the sound, then she looked up at the man again.

"How do you play on all strings at the same time?" she asked.

It seemed to be like playing the lute and the harp at one and the same time. The craftsman gave her a ring for her thumb that held a pick. He instructed her to pick the strings above the fret bar while she pressed the strings to the fret to change the note. She did this and decided that it was much like the lute.

But that was the easy part. With the fingers of the hand that plucked the five strings to make the melody, she had to play chords on the other nineteen strings.

Gwenaelle quickly learned how it was done. She was playing simple tunes in a few moments. She felt a connection with this instrument, which she had never seen before. She had never even seen anything like it. But she felt that she and the instrument were learning each other, and that it would be hers—if she could win it. Now she was determined to compete for this zither, and she felt that she could win it.

She only had to convince her father.

When she finally looked up, it was to see that a crowd had formed around the wood craftsman's tent. They were quiet, watching and listening to her, and it had been easy to ignore them while she had been playing. But now that she had stopped she realized that she was the center of attention.

She wondered if she had done something to bring them— something other than playing well. She wasn't always in complete control of her magic.

She looked over at Judoc to see him watching her with an amused expression on his face. Feeling herself begin to blush, she rolled her eyes at him. She thanked the craftsman, who was smiling openly now. He had a chance to do a lot of business with all the people who had been listening. Gwenaelle gave him back the instrument reluctantly.

All he said was, "You play well."

As they turned to walk back to the castle, she asked Judoc to support her in trying to convince her father that she should compete for the zither. She was sure that her father would allow anything Judoc asked of him, especially now, when Judoc had received the accolade years earlier than anyone had expected.

Judoc hesitated to promise his direct help, however. "Father would commission such an instrument for you, if you asked him," he told her.

Gwenaelle shook her head. "I want that instrument, not one like it." She thought she sounded like a spoiled child at this, so she added, "It spoke to me, Judoc. It wants to be with me as much as I want to have it. It would sing so much better for me than for anyone else."

Judoc looked at her sidewise for a moment. "You talk like it is alive."

"No…" Gwenaelle said hesitantly. "Well, not exactly. Not like you and I are alive."

"Is there another way to be alive?" Judoc asked, raising his eyebrow.

"I know that Grandmother has told you something of this—we both sat through her lectures together." She paused and looked at him hopefully, but he merely looked at her blankly. She laughed ruefully. "All right, so you weren't interested, so it didn't stay with you. But the priests tell of something similar. They talk of God in all things."

Judoc looked startled. He lowered his voice so she could barely hear him, even though there was no one in earshot except themselves and Mari. "Are you saying you think God wants you to have that zither?"

Gwenaelle almost laughed but restrained herself just in time. "Of course not," she said. She also lowered her voice. "I am not so arrogant as that."

Judoc gave her a look that said he was not so sure, but she went on, trying to explain what she felt to someone who could not feel the same.

"It is like there is a spirit in all things—in all things, whether made by man or by God—and I can sometimes feel that spirit." She looked for understanding in Judoc's eyes, but she could see only confusion.

"And this spirit talks to you?" he asked.

Gwenaelle sighed, giving up on him for the moment. "Yes, sort of. Anyway, I believe that zither will not sing as sweetly for anyone else as it would for me."

Judoc smiled down at her. "Sounds like arrogance to me," he said. "And do you think you could win it? Competing against professionals?"

"I think so," Gwenaelle tried to infuse her voice with confidence. She had been confident when she was holding the zither. But that confidence was leaking away from her. She felt the butterflies start flapping their wings in her stomach now. She glanced over at Judoc, to see if he could hear them in her voice.

She heard the laughter bubbling behind his voice as he told her, "I cannot see that father has a prayer in opposing you when you are determined."

"Mistress," Mari spoke for the first time that morning, and both Gwenaelle and Judoc turned to her in surprise. She was pointing down the road, where they could see a plume of dust rising. "Someone comes."

They looked, and Judoc said, "That must be the King. We had better go along to the Duke's court. That is where the Duke will greet the King, and that is where Father will be."

That night, after they had seen the French King arrive but before they retired and while Judoc was still there to side with her, Gwenaelle asked her father for permission to enter the contest for the zither. They were all together in their private sitting room with no one else there. Judoc, Gwenaelle, and her mother and father were all sitting together. Judoc was sewing his jerkin for the morning. Father was polishing his shield. Mother was sewing on the kirtle for Gwenaelle. And Gwenaelle was playing the lute softly, so as not to interrupt their conversation.

Suddenly, Gwenaelle spoke out. "Father," she said, her voice loud in the quiet of the little room. "You know that Lady Katarin has caused a zither to be made as a prize for her competition?"

Father paused as he always did, before speaking. "I had heard of it."

"Judoc and I went to see the zither today." Gwenaelle was glad to hear that she kept her voice even. The butterflies were beginning to dance around in her stomach again, but she couldn't hear even the slightest waver in her voice. "It is the most beautiful instrument."

When Father smiled, Gwenaelle realized that he looked much like Judoc. *Or, perhaps, it is more correct to say that Judoc looks like Father,* she thought to herself. His eyes crinkled in the same way, and he even had a dimple in the same place as Judoc's dimple.

"Hmm," was all he said, although he did not take his eyes away from her.

Now Gwenaelle felt as if there were not enough air for her to breathe. She was breathing faster than usual, but more shallowly—and her heart beat faster and harder against her chest. She made an effort to breathe more deeply and slowly, and felt her heart slow in response. She took an extra deep breath and plunged on. "I want to compete," she said baldly, her chin held up, looking her father in the eye. "I believe I could win that competition."

At that, her father glanced at her mother with no expression on his face. Gwenaelle went on without giving him time to respond.

"You sent me to study with the bards at Carnac," she said. "I am on an equal footing with these troubadours; it is only that I have studied in a different school."

"But, child, women do not compete, here," her father told her gently.

"That's not true, Father," Judoc put in. Gwenaelle could have hugged him, but she did not want to lose the battle that way. "There is a lady troubadour competing this week." He paused and Father looked at him with one eyebrow lifted. He smiled back. "She is the daughter of Lord Roland, Count of Nantes, Lady Corinne."

"And she is competing in a public competition?" Roparzh asked. "I did not think any women did such a thing."

"Oh, yes," Judoc told him. "Most competitions are closed to women, it is true. But there have been women troubadours for a long time. They don't usually travel around, but they compete on an equal footing with the male troubadours."

Gwenaelle held her breath as Roparzh considered this information. She looked at her mother, who had been sewing up until a moment ago, but was now watching her father as well. Oanez looked at Gwenaelle and smiled. Gwenaelle smiled back at her, although she didn't know whether her mother would support her or not.

"So what happens if she wins, this Lady Corinne?" Roparzh asked. He glanced over at Gwenaelle, too, but he didn't smile. "Does she stay and write music for the Duke and Duchess?"

"Yes, I would imagine she would," Judoc responded calmly. "She would be protected, here, you know. Since the Duke is your half-brother, I imagine that he would take even greater care of your daughter, should she win."

"Gwenaelle and Judoc together might win allies, here," Oanez spoke softly, but Roparzh turned to her immediately. He always listened to Oanez. "I know you have been concerned about how we are seen in the larger world for some time."

Roparzh nodded, thinking about her words and Judoc's. He looked at Gwenaelle searchingly, as if he were trying to see into the future. Gwenaelle looked back at him, hoping desperately that he would decide in her favor.

"It is true," Roparzh said, finally. "Alan knows he can count on me, but I have not come to wait upon him for some time. The land has been peaceful, and I have allowed my concern for my own land and people to keep me away from Rennes for several years. This may have been a mistake."

"I don't understand," Gwenaelle said. Her father was talking about the reason he had been so serious lately. "How can it be wrong to take care of your people, when you are taking care of them for Duke Alan?"

Roparzh smiled tiredly. "Of course, that is not wrong. The problem comes from not being visible, here."

Gwenaelle did not understand this, so she just nodded for him to continue.

"While I was taking such good care of his people at home, others have been here, trying to insinuate themselves into the Duke's favor." He grimaced. "At my expense, perhaps. I have seen some things which make me think this could be so."

"But with Judoc being here…" Gwenaelle prompted him.

"Judoc has been doing something towards alleviating this situation," Roparzh admitted, smiling over at his son.

"Gwenaelle could become friends with Katarin," Judoc said, suddenly. "I think she would be glad of someone close to her own age."

"That's very true," Oanez said. "Katarin has only been married to Alan for a year, and we do not know her as we knew Franseza. She seems to be very much on her best behavior, with all of the nobles being here. I am sure she would be glad to have someone she could relax with."

Roparzh nodded thoughtfully. He looked over at Gwenaelle searchingly. "All right," he said. "You can compete in this musical competition."

Gwenaelle nearly cheered aloud. She only stopped herself because she thought her father would see that as too childish. Instead, she stood up and went to kiss his cheek.

"Thank you, father," she said. She couldn't keep the smile off her face.

For the next two days, Gwenaelle spent all her time choosing and then practicing the songs she would play and sing for the competition. She only went out twice, to watch Judoc jousting and to cheer him when he won. She was very glad that he did not joust any more than this, as she sat in the stands with her heart in her mouth the entire time.

True to Judoc's words to her, the men did not fight with blunted weapons. She saw many injuries while she watched, although only one fatality. She understood that they needed to practice, to keep sharp and in shape. But she thought, very privately indeed, that they could stay just as sharp if they used blunted weapons.

Judoc did seem to be a rather good knight. He won both of the times he took the field, and he came back with nothing more than bruises. One of his good friends was not so fortunate. Gwenaelle saw him carried off the field, alive but possibly crippled for life. All of the knights and squires seemed to take this possibility in stride, but she noticed that none of them looked at the young man after he fell.

The troubadour competition was to be on the last day of the tournament. Finally, that day arrived. Gwenaelle was nervous from the moment she woke up in the morning. The amount of time she had to wait seemed too long, but then, seemingly the next moment, she had no time left at all. She had difficulty settling to any task, and even attending to what was said to her was sometimes beyond her. Finally, Oanez got her attention by laughing at her.

She stopped her pacing and looked at her mother contritely. "I'm sorry, Mother," she said. She sat down and gave her attention to what Oanez was saying.

"I have finished your new kirtle," Oanez told her patiently. "I thought you could wear it tonight."

Oanez brought out the kirtle and held it up for Gwenaelle to see. On the background of deep green, Oanez had embroidered a lovely garden scene. There were all the wonders of nature together. There was a tree in the center, with different flowers around it. And there, behind the tree, peeked out a faun. And above, in the branches of the tree, squirrels played.

"Oh!" Gwenaelle exclaimed when she had looked at it for a few moments. "It is lovely! Of course, I'll wear it."

"Well, then, go and put it on," Oanez told her. "Then we can go down to the Great Hall."

Gwenaelle laughed and took the kirtle in to have Mari help her put it on. She was ready in ten minutes, and it took them ten more to reach the Great Hall.

The Great Hall was already busy, with many of the guests standing around, talking to each other and waiting for the Duke and the King to arrive. They couldn't see Roparzh. Neither of them were tall, and there were many tall men in the way. They looked at one another in despair for a moment, then they went in and began to make their way through the crowd.

Gwenaelle found the Lord Chamberlain, Lord Robert, near the high table and identified herself to him. He was a fussy little man, barely taller than she was herself. He looked flustered at the confusion that reigned in his domain, and at the same time as if he were proud of it. He took her into an alcove that had been partitioned off from the rest of the great hall with several large tapestries.

There were several men and one woman in the alcove when Gwenaelle went in. Each one was alone, although they were severely crowded in that portion of a room. Each of the troubadours was either tuning his instrument, singing softly to himself, or just standing with his eyes closed.

Gwenaelle found a portion of the alcove that was not occupied, and she went and stood there, waiting for the announcement. She looked around surreptitiously, wondering if any of these people could be as nervous as she was. Most of them were older, and she supposed that they had done this before, many times. Yet they still avoided talking to one another—many of them looked surly, as if they expected others to try to speak to them.

Lord Robert called for attention, and he got it almost immediately. "Once the Duke and the King have both arrived—they should be here in about half an hour—I will begin calling for you to come out individually," Lord Robert said. He pinned a long paper onto one of the tapestries. "Here is the order in which you will be called. Pay attention. You will not be given a second chance if you do not come out when called."

He waited a moment, to see if there were any questions. When all of the troubadours merely stared at him, he moved aside the tapestry and went back out to the great hall. As soon as he was gone, there was a concerted move toward the notice.

"We are to be bracketed by our ladies," said one of the men. "The lady Corinne will play first, and the lady Gwenaelle will play last."

They all turned to look at Gwenaelle, even Lady Corinne. Gwenaelle said nothing, merely looked back at them, waiting to see if any of them would try to intimidate her. She was the newcomer, here. But, after a moment of staring at her, they all turned away.

At Carnac, they would have tried to intimidate the newcomer, but then again, the school at Carnac had been well-established. She was thinking of the students at the school. These were not students of the same teachers; they were professionals hoping to win a job.

It felt like an interminable time before Lord Robert called the first name, but Gwenaelle expected it was really less than an hour. As soon as the first name was called, silence descended upon the rest of them. They watched Lady Corinne move out of the alcove with her head held high. As soon as she was gone, most of them went back to practicing fingerings or singing their songs under their breaths.

Gwenaelle stood in the corner and meditated. She could barely hear the other musicians outside the alcove. She could also hear the noise of the diners which continued, unabated, throughout the playing. As the evening wore on, and the other musicians were called to play for the Duke, Gwenaelle stood alone.

It became easier to be alone since the musicians did not return after their turns. Gwenaelle supposed that they went off to eat their dinners—or to drink them, whichever they preferred.

Finally, Gwenaelle was alone in the alcove. She heard her name called outside the alcove.

In a meditative trance, Gwenaelle walked out of the alcove to the space between the dais which held the high table and the lower tables. She saw Duchess Katarin looking at her, and the Duke and the King ignoring her. Katarin smiled at her, and Gwenaelle curtseyed.

The next moment, still in her trance, Gwenaelle was playing. She played her own tune, which she had written for her teachers at Carnac. And she sang an abbreviated version of Pwyll's adventures in Annwn.

As she began singing, only Katarin was paying attention. She sang of the hunt, and of how Pwyll became separated from his nobles. She sang of how he followed his hounds until they came upon the hounds of Annwn with their own kill, and he took their kill away from them.

As she sang of the appearance of Arawn, King of Annwn, the Underworld, she noticed that the Duke was listening. The room seemed a little bit quieter. Arawn, she sings, is greatly offended by what Pwyll has done—she feels the emotions of those who listened as they empathize with Arawn.

The Great Hall became quieter still, as she sings of the compensation that Pwyll gives to Arawn; he agrees to take Arawn's form for a year in order to defeat Arawn's enemy for him. Gwenaelle sings of Pwyll's chastity while he sleeps next to Arawn's beautiful queen for a year.

By the time Gwenaelle sang of the battle between Pwyll and Arawn's enemy, the hall was silent. Everyone was listening. She ended the tale by telling how, when Arawn returned to his home, his wife asked him what had been the matter with him for a year, and he realized that Pwyll had been even more honorable than he had expected.

The hall remained silent for a moment after Gwenaelle finished her song, then thunderous applause broke out everywhere. Gwenaelle stood there, basking in the applause.

Finally, the Duke stood up and signaled an end to the ovation. "I believe," he said, smiling at Gwenaelle and then at the audience. "I believe that we have a clear winner. Is that not so, my dear?" He turned to look at Katarin, who stood up as well.

"Indeed, I believe you are right," Katarin called for the zither, which was to be the prize. And she called Gwenaelle up to the high table to accept her winnings. "And along with the zither, Gwenaelle will become the official troubadour of Brittany."

Gwenaelle accepted the zither joyfully. She could almost feel her joy returned from the zither as she took it in her arms. She was more sure than ever that they belonged to each other, and that they belonged here, in the court of Brittany.

Sir Blodry The Sentry

DJ Tyrer

Sometimes, Sir Blodry did not enjoy being a Knight of the Round Table; so much was expected of him! King Arthur did not like to see Knights spent in idleness, so would insist on them going out on quests, patrolling the coasts on the look-out for mauraders and generally maintaining the security of the kingdom. Blodry was not at all suited to such tasks, being the sort of knight who excelled at the feasting side of things rather than the martial. Being, unfortunately, tender-hearted, Blodry was not one to relish violence, yet somehow, through an unfeasible chain of coincidences that even he found incredible, had managed to give the impression of being a competent and valorous warrior. Although such unintentional success brought fame and fortune, it also raised expectations. So, it should come as no surprise that, despite not enjoying his current task, Blodry was grateful it was a nice, simple, straightforward one.

Sir Blodry had been sent north to garrison a strategic fort. Such was Arthur's confidence in him that he considered Blodry, alone, the equal of a medium-sized garrison. He had not appreciated the compliment, as it was not only a huge responsibility, but meant he was left all on his own in a rather spooky fortification—that had started out as a hillfort in some ancient time before the Romans had built an outpost to hold back the Picts—which had become a priory before Arthur, in his turn, had repaired it after he had restored the kingdom to order. Not that the repair had extended to actually making the place comfortable; his bed was a pile of straw in the corner of a draughty room with a roof that looked as if it would leak should the weather turn to rain.

The daytime wasn't too bad as he could spend his days in the sun, but the night saw him barricaded into the barracks, jumping every time a bat flapped past or an owl hooted in the distance. He really disliked the night.

It was on his fourth night there that it happened. Blodry had been cowering as usual upon his bed of straw, fending off the attentions of an overly-inquisitive moth, when he heard a sudden sound from the courtyard at the centre of the fort; it was the sound of chains clanking. Not a sound you were likely to hear outside of a prison, he did not think the rattling sound boded well. Worst of all, he knew that it was his duty to investigate.

Duty and desire warred within Blodry as he buried his face into the straw, hoping that the sound might cease. Clutching literally at straws, he would gratefully have grasped any of the metaphorical variety that might have offered him a way out of the situation. None came, and the noise continued, leaving him no choice but to do his duty or cave-in to cowardice.

With a sigh, he rose from his makeshift bed and fumbled about for his sword in the shadows of the room. Finding it, he rose and tiptoed to the door, still half-hoping that the sounds might stop and allow him the opportunity to shirk his sentry duties. Still, the chains insisted on continuing to clank.

His heart felt not only as if it were in his mouth, but halfway down his chin as it attempted to make its escape. He swallowed hard, just in case a heart really could get out, and went to the door. The clanking chains sounded almost as if they were right outside. He raised his sword ready as he lifted away the bar that held the door shut.

"Have at thee!" he cried, voice quavering, as he flung the door open.

"Rarghh!" replied the ghostly figure that was rattling the chains.

Brave sir knight shrieked in a very unbrave manner and slammed the door shut upon the hideous sight, nearly dropping his sword as he did so. Unfortunately, he did not have the chance to replace the bar before it burst open and the frightful entity entered.

The ghost was like a skinny old man with long wild hair and dressed in the habit of a monk; it was not a very good habit, being tattered and torn. The sound of chains was due to the fact that it—or was it a he?—was wrapped around in chains which it held in its hands and shook as if in a rage.

"Rarghh!" it repeated, rattling its chains for emphasis.

Blodry very nearly fainted, his sword slipping from his fingers.

"What do you want?" he wailed at the spectre. "Leave me alone!"

"Rarghh!" it replied. The roar was starting to become irritating rather than terrifying.

"I don't understand! What do you want me to do?"

It said: "Rarghh!" again and shook its chains at him once more. Suddenly, realisation dawned.

"It's the chains, isn't it?"

"Rarghh!" it cried in a particularly emphatic manner.

"Let me help you," said Blodry. Unfortunately, it was an offer easily made but not so easily followed through on; the chains were so tightly bound about the hapless ghost that he could not work out how to free it. No matter how Blodry tugged or pulled, the chains stayed wound about the ghost's insubstantial form. Sadly, the seeming lack of solidity did not allow him to just pull the chains through the ghost's body.

"Rarghh!" it cried, plaintively.

"Oh, wait, I have an idea!" Sometimes Blodry tried so hard to avoid doing anything related to his knight job that he forgot he was a knight. He grabbed up his sword and told the ghost to hold the chains against the doorframe saying, "Hold them firm!"

Raising his sword, Blodry brought it down in a mighty blow that shattered the links of the chain. It didn't do the blade much good, but that was the least of his concerns at this particular moment. Smashed, the chains fell away from the ghostly monk, releasing it.

With a mighty wheeze that startled Blodry and caused him to drop his sword once more in fright, the ghost sucked in its breath. Then, it spoke: "Oh, my, thank you! Oh, it is nice not to be constricted anymore! Thank you! Thank you!"

"Um, you're welcome." Beaming wildly, the ghost no longer seemed scary at all. "So, ah, how did you end up covered in chains like that?"

"Oh, the usual way, I"m afraid. I was a monk in life, back when this fort was a priory, and didn't do very well at keeping my vows – you know, poverty and such like – and, so, I was punished by being bound here in a most literal sense. But, thanks to you, I am free to move on to the next stage of... life. I really am very grateful!" And, with that, it vanished, leaving Blodry alone in the darkness.

An owl hooted in the distance, but he didn't feel quite as afraid as he had before. In fact, Blodry felt quite pleased with himself; this stint as a sentry didn't seem quite as bad as it had done – and, he would have a great story to tell when he returned to court. Suitably edited, of course!

Clipart by AnimalsClipart.com

The Bluebells of Bonny Forest

Cynthia Morrison

The blooming daffodils painted a brilliant splash of welcomed color as spring began to peek out amongst the valley surrounding Chase Manor. Sir Chase stepped out onto his bedroom balcony to summon his Squire to ready his steed for jousting practice in the arena. The 1170 tournament season of King Henry II was beginning in only a week. Chase then made his way downstairs where he enjoyed his breakfast of eggs, ham and honey bread which featured a recipe left behind by ancient Roman invaders. With a hearty release of a belch, he stood addressing his maid and exclaimed

"Well done maid! Now to hit my mark. In the arena of course."

"That you shall Sir. Of this, I have no doubt."

"That makes one of us."

Maid Mary bent a knee and gave her curtsy as her lord of the manor exited in amusement of his own comments. Dry humor happened to be one of his prominent characteristics along with an underlying streak of a viper. She learned quickly how to dodge and avoid the latter. Too bad for Chase's suitors that didn't share Mary's intuitions. But then again, he never intended that they should take his name anyway.

After Chase had tested the saddle girth for security, he mounted his best warhorse, Mace. Away they cantered into the morning mist. Chase preferred to get the dickens out of his warhorse before they entered practice so the horse could focus better on the task at hand. This training method has almost always paid off for him in the past. Squire Garth rhythmically tossed the metal rings in the air upon Sir Chase's approach at a gallop.

"How many is that Garth?"

"You've speared thirty-four rings so far Sir."

"We'll give Mace a short rest then start on the Quintain."

"Aye Sir, I'll take him to water."

Chase walked to the rear of the stables where he viewed the fair maiden in the field collecting wild berries for the evening meal. He reminded himself that he needed to find out more about her so he could plan the release of his underlying viper he was so infamous for. Looking out onto the vast land that surrounded his estate he placed his foot on the holding pen rail in an attempt to massage away the knee joint pain caused by jousting injuries of days gone by. Chase entered the tool room where medicines were stored in search of the salve that Garth normally applies to Mace's swollen knee due to a jumping accident. The injury has a tendency to reappear under certain weather conditions. Chase stepped back outside to inquire about the medicine.

"Garth, where do you keep the knee salve for Mace?"

"I've used it all Sir. We are in need of more."

"Very well, tie up Mace and ready Coal Tar for a journey to the village so I may replenish our supply from the blacksmith."

"Right away Sir."

Chase and Coal Tar made their way along the country road where the sounds of singing robins accompanied them. The season was still too early to present the landscape of bluebell flowers that typically carpet the floor of Bonny

Forest. Chase slowed Coal Tar's pace as he reminisced of days gone by in the woods. He promised himself that he will give a tour to his berry picking maiden after his victory at the upcoming tournament and share with her the blue gleaming buds. Along with an evil grin, the dusty boot heel gave a punch to Coal Tar's side and away they went to make their purchase.

The trumpets roared as did the crowd on opening tournament day. King Henry II was abroad so the knights who entered the tournament were given a chance to vote on the events of the day. Shall it be a one to one Joust, skill at arms or melee? It seemed that spring had sprung not only flowers but heightened egos as the choice was to combat in Melee. Perhaps it was the Irish coffee for breakfast. Nonetheless, the melee was known as the most violent and merciless of all the events. This event usually ended in total mayhem, as there are no barriers for the warhorses with their riders tending to use more hurtful circumstances towards their opponents. All entrants are on the field of honor to combat each other all at once. Chase noticed Sir Belford and rode across the field to greet him.

"Greetings Sir Belford. This day finds you fit and well I pray."

"Ah, Sir Chase good to see you with Mace once again. I trust you both recovered from last season?"

"As well as we could. Of course, we both now use the same knee medicine mixture."

"I was wondering if the horse odor was Mace or you old man."

Both men were amused by Belford's attempt to calm the anticipation facing them.

"I say, Belford, you see that we have a Frenchman joining us today."

"I wouldn't be too concerned about him. His name is Sir Regis of Lyon. I was watching him late last night as he was secretly walking up and down on his lances to crack them in hopes of easier shattering for the broken lance point system. Little did he know we would be at Melee instead of inside the tilting list ha!"

"Well done Sir Belford. He's probably sweating pebbles by now."

"I"m sure he is. Are you well ready for combat Sir Chase?"

"That we are Sir."

Just at that moment the tournament trumpets called for the knight's to enter the field. A squire can never seem to move fast enough when his master requires a weapon and shield. Garth dodged through the other ground assistants almost as if it were he in avoidance of destruction himself. After delivering lance and shield to Chase, he held Mace in position until the Herald gave command to commence fair play upon the field.

"At the ready. Alle!"

The Herald's enthusiastic command to start the melee had set the sounds of stress-ridden leather against equine muscle into a forward motion of no return. There was no stopping them now. At various intervals, the knight's clashed weapons against shield and armor. The field suddenly transformed into one big tempest riddled with unorganized harmful intent. The eleven fighting men took on a surreal comparison to that of birds in pursuit of nest hunting predators. Sir Chase set his aim on the visiting Frenchman, who chose the morning star as a weapon. Chase directed Mace at the foreigner on full charge. Chase was certain that his lance would certainly unhorse the French knight since he had a five-foot advantage in weapon length. Mace's nostrils expanded and contracted as he headed for the black French stallion. The crowd roared, but the men only heard themselves within the mighty helms that crowned their heads. Sir Chase lowered his lance into place and took aim. Only a couple of feet from impact Sir Regis slung his morning star that clashed with Chase's helm. One of the spiked metal balls found its way under the helm's bottom ridge hitting Chase's chin like an Olympic boxer. The blow threw Chase's head in a backward motion causing loss of balance creating a departure from his seat upon Mace. Chase was now lying dazed on the tiltyard floor.

Valor was the intended presence in the lush green valley as the sun rays beamed down on the field as if to offer their blessing. The ribcage that God had kept for man was no longer complete as one part. Why do we see the Stars with eyes clenched so tightly from excruciating circumstance? Heavy hooves passed as Chase attempted to regain conscience.

True, the mighty had fallen. As Chase waited for painless breath, he was comforted by the blueness of sky through the visor of his helm. Heavy hooves passed once again. Then an unfamiliar voice penetrated the cold steel of his helm.

"You foolish charger. You fight with no purpose. What did this fair skin warrior do to you that you must ride in decisive engagement against him with lance and shield? Have you no respect for the meaning of War? Is battle such a game simply to entertain those who beg entertainment by self-destruction?"

With his hand still clenched onto the shield, Chase gazed through the eye slit of his helm to find the voice. A mountainous male figure appeared who was clad in the armor of antiquity with chiseled facial features framed by a beard. The figure held a spear of Romans past. Sir Chase then managed to regain enough breath to push out his reply

"Sport."

The mysterious figure squinted his eyes in deep curiosity then responded to Chase's comment.

"Sport?!"

Managing another breath Chase inquired

"And who are you?"

The mountainous figure gave a hearty laugh and exclaimed

"But I am MARS, god of war. But you would not recognize such a presence if you chose combat as a sport then would you charge?"

Mars went on to explain that Chase should spare himself from further injury and that he should train dogs. Fighting dogs such as the ancient warriors did that ran under the bellies of war horses to confuse them and put opponents off balance.

Suddenly, his almost divine presence vanished as quickly as it appeared.

"Are you hurt Sir!?, let me take the helmet from you. Just hold still and stay where you are."

This was the familiar voice of Squire Garth. Chase immediately inquired about the mysterious entity

"Where is Mars."

"Mars Sir? What Mars?"

"The Mars that was just here. You know, MARS, the God of War!"

"Sir, I read the registry this morning, and I don't remember any Sir Mars competing on this day. Stay put if you will Sir, you've hit your head in the fall."

But Sir Chase continued his desperate plea to find Mars.

"Mars. Mars. Where did he go? You must find him, Garth. Find Mars."

Just then the tournament medical team arrived to carry Chase off the field.

"I'll make my way to seek this Sir Mars and then meet you in the pavilion."

Garth searched high and low asking if anyone was familiar with Sir Mars but to no avail. Some of the event attendees were even amused at Garth's inquiry especially those who were obviously educated about the ancient worlds. Shock had overtaken Sir Chase's physical state as he traveled by stretcher to a doctor's pavilion where threads then held his flesh on mend. His cracked ribcage would not allow him to support armor for another 8 weeks. They say he wouldn't let go of his delusional moments he had with someone named Mars. But Chase was certain that Mars was real. Divine or not, Mars spoke, and Chase listened. He gave heed to Mar's sensible words but with only one exception. An exception of revenge on the Frenchman who dared unhorse him on this day! Chase made a personal vow that when he was mended physically, he would make way to Lyon, France to even the score.

Throughout his recovery, Chase would often gaze out of his bedchamber window. Garth continued to train and ready Mace for the next planned adventure. Chase noticed too much emphasis on a certain maneuver where the horse would raise off its front feet and lunge into the opponent's approach.

"Not too much on the lunge.

I don't want Mace getting too use to that one."

Garth waved to his master in acknowledgement. Chase lifted his spyglass to investigate closer the efforts of his newly found berry gathering maiden. He decided to extend his vow with regard to his journey to France. His additional vow reinforced that upon his return from his victory in France that he would introduce this maiden to the carpet of bluebells that blanket the Bonny forest floor. The bluebells are the true Herald of an English countryside spring. Just then the maid Mary knocked at his bedchamber door with nourishment for the broken warrior Lord of the manor.

Several weeks later found Squire Garth mounting coal tar along with weapons of combat. Sir Chase gave maid Mary a reassuring arm around her shoulder and a few inspiring words.

"Now Mary, Uncle William's serf will be along today to stay and assist you while we are on quest. He's been given strict instructions to follow your every request."

Chase mounted Mace and away the men went to catch the ferry crossing to France. Mace and Coal Tar came to a halt in the fortress's field where the duel should take place. Both Sir Chase and Sir Regis agreed to let the chance of a thrown coin choose weapons. The Farthing landed in Sir Chase's favor that secured the duel shall involve lance and shield. Sir Regis beckoned for his squire to fetch his lance and shield. Sir Chase intervened.

"Pardon Moi Sir Regis. To have this match on equal circumstance would require the lance to be of the same wood as well as craftsman. Therefore, I summon my squire to deliver you one of my lances if you will."

Sir Regis knew that if he challenged Chase's request, then he would be considered an unfair challenger. He agreed and was armed by Garth. Chase began to psychologically prepare himself for victory by envisioning a Falcon in pursuit of a sparrow. With Sir Regis representing the sparrow of course. Both men and war horses in position at opposite ends of the field. The village Herald dropped the flag.

"Alle!"

The sound of clattering hooves filled the inside of the courtyard walls. Mace began to snort at the approaching French stallion as he remembered the steed from the last tournament. Regis at a loss for points now with a solid lance devised a plan to unhorse Chase by ringing the "tower bell". That term being slang for the area just below the crest on top of the knight's helm. An educated combatant knows all too soon that wherever the head goes, the body is sure to follow. That is if the head is still attached. Only seconds before impact Sir Regis pulled his lance upward to hit high. With no time for command, Mace decided to engage his rear and lunge technique that Garth so dearly enjoyed enforcing. Although Mace was not directed to utilize the maneuver, this happened to save Chase by bringing his shield in line with the high lance aim by Regis. Both combatants stopped at their ends of the list. Regis tilted his helm backwards enough to be heard when he exclaimed to Chase

"Cleverly trained horse you have there Sir Chase."

Chase amused, pushed his helm back as well to reply, "Oui Monsieur, I know."

This time, Chase decided to drop his chivalrous manners to become equal with his scrupulous competitor. The flag dropped. The war horses galloped once again. Suddenly Chase dropped his shield and raised his arm as a bird would it's wing. Sir Regis found his lance being captured inside Sir Chase's armpit as Chase then lowered his arm to grasp Regis" lance. Regis was unable to keep his weapon that was causing loss of his seating so he released his lance which put him at a five-point disadvantage. He knew he had been defeated by the English knight so he dismounted his black stallion and gave a salute to Chase without words and returned back into his countryside castle. Squire Garth was filled with joy and celebration.

"Well done Sir Chase!"

"Yes Garth and with gratitude for your lunge training with Mace,

I survived the rat bastard knight's attempt to ring my bell!"

Sir Chase gave Garth a victory embrace with a pat on the shoulders.

"Let us eat, drink and be merry then slumber this night. For in the morrow, we shall return to the bluebells of Bonny Forest where ye shall begin constructing pens to train dogs for battle."

The Nameless Knight

DJ Tyrer

The pennants fluttered gaily above the lists as the crowds gathered to celebrate the New Year with the Lady Day tournament. Hawkers let out cries to advertise their wares, sweetmeats, and pies, as the crowds surged by to take their seats or stand pressed together at the fringe. Arrayed in shining armour that reflected the sun like polished mirrors and brightly-coloured tabards, the knights rode out to be greeted with cheers and whistles.

Having paraded past the crowds, they each approached the King one at a time to offer their good faith and receive his blessing in turn. Then, they returned to their respective ends to await their moment of glory or defeat.

Sir Escalon and Sir Thomas de Courci were the first to joust, spurring their horses forward in a thundering charge.

Lances lowered, each took aim at the other knight's shield, and they met with a crash. Lance tips shattered and both warriors shuddered in their saddles, but neither fell.

Reaching the end of the lists, they wheeled and halted, their mounts pawing at the ground, impatient to charge again, enthused by the excitement of the crowd. Squires ran up to take the splintered lances and pass fresh ones to their masters.

At the King's command, the knights charged again. This time, Sir Escalon shifted slightly in his saddle so that de Courci"s lance struck his shield the lightest of blows. His smashed Sir Thomas straight in the chest, shattering and throwing the man to the dusty earth. Cheers and jeers rose in equal measure, drowning out the fallen knight's howl of pain.

Sir Thomas's squire ran forward to his master, who lay still upon the ground and wrenched his helmet free to reveal a jagged splinter of wood embedded in his eye and blood patterning his face. Further cheers and cries of concern went up at the sight. Men ran forward to help carry him off the field; there was every chance that, while his eye was likely lost, his life could be saved.

A murmuration ran through the crowd as they discussed the odds of the Knight's survival and the prospect of further such bloody entertainment.

Sir Robert de Brusi and Sir Jambres de l'Isle were the next to ride against one another and provided further entertainment, Sir Robert unhorsing Sir Jambres only to yield in turn as they fought on foot.

The tournament was interrupted and a fearful silence descended upon the scene as a knight in black armour with a black shield and mounted upon a great black horse rode unbidden onto the field. Black armour was not unknown, if unusual, but none had seen armour quite so black; nor had they seen a horse as black; nor one clotted about its frothing jaws and blade-sharp hooves with blood. To the crowd, it was as if some knight errant of the damned had ridden forth from Hell to offer a challenge.

And, a challenge was offered.

The King rose and demanded to know who the knight was.

Visor still down, the knight turned his head a little way towards the King, his only acknowledgement.

"I have come to challenge the best men of your kingdom," came a hollow voice from the echo chamber of his great helm.

"And, why should I bother with one such as you?" asked the King, barely keeping the sneer out of his voice. "Why should I not command my men to fall upon you and slaughter you like a dog?"

The voice was a monotone, devoid of fear or passion, as the Knight declared, "All at once or one at a time, it makes no difference to me: I shall slay them all. I have fought a thousand knights and not one lives to recall our battle."

"You are certainly brave," said the King, his tone no longer sneering, if not particularly welcoming. "What is it you desire?"

"I will fight your men, all your knights, and if any of them can defeat me, you shall receive a boon such as no other king shall know."

"Which would be...?"

"Eternal life and eternal fertility for your kingdom."

The King laughed, disbelievingly. "And, what would you have in return? My soul?"

"No."

"Then, what?"

The helm turned a little further to look to the King's left. "If I defeat all your knights here today, you shall give me your daughter, body and soul, forever."

The King laughed as if the knight in black armour were a jester clowning for him. "Very well."

"Father!"

He turned to his daughter and patted her arm. "Do not distress yourself, my dear. This is a madman, not a devil, and my men will make short work of him."

Despite his confidence, she wrung her hands as the nameless knight declared there would be no quarter and rode to one end to await his first opponent.

"Go," called the King and Sir Escalon and the knight in black armour charged one another, hooves thundering across the ground.

Their lances struck home, but while the nameless knight barely seemed to sway in his saddle, Sir Escalon was thrown to the ground.

The knight wheeled his coal-black steed about and rode it over the fallen Sir Escalon, trampling him into the dust and leaving him a battered and bloodied mess.

Sir Robert de Brusi and Sir Jambres de l'Isle fell in like manner. Then, disdaining honour in favour of expediency, Sir Lionel de Leon aimed his lance at the nameless knight's visor, hoping to penetrate the brain. But, while the lance struck home and shattered into a shower of fragments, none seemed to pass through the narrow eye-slit, while Sir Lionel was unhorsed and ridden down in his turn.

Fully two-dozen knights and more rode against the knight in black armour. Not one kept his saddle nor survived the encounter.

The King sat and stared in a mixture of horror and amazement at the slaughter that had overtaken the flower of chivalry in his kingdom. Beside him, his daughter sobbed at the thought of what must now befall her.

"Is that all?" the knight in black armour asked, voice as uninflected as ever. "Do you have no more knights who would die in your name?"

"No," sobbed the King. "You have killed them all."

"Then, I shall take my prize."

"Wait!" exclaimed the princess. "If I am to be yours forever more, I would see the face of the man who would claim me."

"I do not remove my helmet in daylight," he replied. "Now, come."

"No, not now. If I am to be yours, I would see your face. Come to me tonight and show me your face by moonlight and, then, I shall go with you."

"Very well. I shall return tonight. But, do not think to resist me: no castle, no army can stand against me. You shall be mine, regardless, but many more would die."

"I will not resist you," said the King; "I am a man of my word. I am a king."

"Kings are seldom the most honest of men," proclaimed the knight, wheeling his horse and riding away, leaving the watching crowd in a stunned silence.

The King was as good as his word and made no attempt to hide or protect his daughter, but placed her in the courtyard with the gates open to await the Knight's return.

Night fell and a gibbous moon illuminated the courtyard as she waited, pacing nervously.

She halted and cocked his head as she heard the distant sound of hoofbeats. The sound grew nearer and, then, she saw the black-armoured knight framed in the gateway. The horse reared and whinnied and, then, the knights rode into the courtyard and stopped a short distance from her.

The knight swung himself down from his saddle and stood before her.

"Show me your face," she whispered, voice quavering with fear.

He reached up and gripped his helm and wrenched it from his shoulders. The princess screamed. The face that looked at her was that of a corpse, gaunt and ghastly, with eyes that blazed with the very fires of hell.

"You have seen me," it said; "now, come with me."

It held out a hand towards her.

The princess stepped forward with an air of reluctance and began to raise her hand as if to take the one it proffered, then swung it up towards its head and stabbed a slender blade into its throat.

A mirthless laugh greeted the blow. "Do not imagine that you can slay me, child, for I am immortal."

She sagged. The knight looked dispassionately down at her with eyes like burning coals.

Behind it, unnoticed, a shadow detached itself from the darkness of the castle wall and approached silently.

"Come," said the knight, reaching for her.

She danced back and, in that instant, a blow smashed into the Knight, and it fell to its knees. Behind it, a bloodied bandaged stretched taut across his eye socket, stood Sir Thomas de Courci, the last living knight in the kingdom. He raised his sword and swung it against the Knight's neck, shearing its terrifying head from its shoulders with a blade blessed by a priest.

The skull bounced away, the eyes extinguishing while the body collapsed with a clatter. The horse let out a keening howl and vanished in a blaze of flames that left a whiff of sulphur in the air.

Within moments, the armour tarnished and collapsed and the body within transformed into dust, scattering across the courtyard on the breeze, the skull likewise.

"Thank you – oh, thank you!" she cried and threw herself into his arms.

He hugged her, but made no demands upon her, already having a wife of his own.

"All I did is do my duty," he said, "and fulfil my vows to your father. Now, if you do not object, I really could do with further rest." He leant upon his sword and rubbed at his bandage, then yawned. "I think you owe the priest more thanks than you do me."

The Sorrows of Fainwen: The Fall of Camelot

Ben Fine

The Coming of Mordred

Fainwen's body ached as the tournament concluded. It had been a large competition, and he jousted against seven knights, unseating them all. They were all younger, strong and foolish, but not very skilled. Fainwen could handle them easily. He had been a warrior all his life and had been with King Arthur since the beginning. Now so many of the old fellowship had died, and they were replaced by younger men, who had never been tested in real combat. These new soldiers enjoyed the tournaments, but Fainwen felt that these fake combats were silly and unnecessary. Still, he had to participate and exhibit his skill, or else the younger men would think he was too old and his fighting days were over.

He often talked about this with his close friend Lancelot, the greatest of the warriors, and the Breton essentially felt the same; but he too kept on competing.

Arthur had been victorious in his many wars, and his enemies had been defeated. He united the Britons and kept the Saxons and Angles trapped in their eastern enclaves. Peace had reigned in Great Britain, for the most part, for thirty years. Yet now Arthur seemed tired. The departure of Merlin had left him rudderless and, perhaps goaded by his queen, Guenevere, he turned to the Christian Bishops in Londinium. He was rapidly abandoning the old ways and the old magic for the new god Jesus and a rift formed among his Fellowship.

Jesus promised an eternal salvation, yet for the traditional Briton, life was based on warfare. A warrior Celt relied on the protection of magic by the Druid priests and priestesses and for those who still adhered to the old religion, eternal salvation meant little. In the court of King Arthur two factions began to slowly emerge; those who kept the old ways and the old religion and those who chose to follow Christianity and all that the new religion demanded.

When Merlin followed his love Nimue and never returned, Arthur began to listen to the Christian bishops. As the King turned to this new strange God, the protection of the Great Goddess, and the protection of Merlin's magic fell away. Without Merlin and magic, the Fellowship began to crumble.

Fainwen often thought of the Fellowship and the great part it had played in his life. He had abandoned his ancestral lands in North Wales to follow the great Briton, King Arthur. Ryence, his overlord, the king of North Wales, was an enemy of Arthur's, and hence an enemy of Fainwen. Although Fainwen still held his own Welsh lands, and thus had Ryence formally as his liege, it was Fainwen's brother Fay who lived in the familial manor house. Fainwen had not returned to his childhood home in years, and now he was alone. His wife and his sons were dead, and his daughter was married to a wealthy Roman-Briton, Maneboris, who lived near the old Roman city of Mantorious. He had three grandchildren that he rarely saw and regretfully accepted that as part of the life of a soldier.

Fainwen had seen the growth of Camelot in good times and bad. As a lad of just fourteen, his father Sir Bangar took him to the festival at Winchester to honor the Great Goddess and perhaps choose a new war chieftain. The powerful Uther Pendragon had been the last to unite many of the Britons and at that time, the Celts were more interested in fighting each other than in driving out the German invaders. The Welsh, secure in their hilly homeland did not view fighting the Saxons as urgently as did the Britons of the lowlands.

Over the years, the Christians co-opted the Festival to the Great Goddess and called it Pentecost, but when Fainwen was a boy, all the Britons went to honor the Great Goddess, either at Winchester or at the Stone Circle at Stonehenge. At Winchester that year, standing in the crowd, Fainwen had heard the uproar when the young boy Artorius, supposedly the son of Sir Ector, pulled a sword from the stone. Fainwen had not seen it happen, but his father believed that it did. Bangar and Fainwen then pledged allegiance to the new king, Arthur, who was acknowledged by many, but not all, as the son of Uther.

Fainwen became his father's squire and together they fought alongside Arthur against the eleven kings. As Arthur's rivals fell one by one, in battle after battle, Fainwen saw the young king unite the Britons. Only the north of Wales, Cornwall, Scotland and the eastern lands remained outside the realm of Arthur.

Fainwen then fought alongside Arthur at the Battle of Badon Hill. The Saxons, originally invited by Vortigern to settle in Britain, lived in villages on the east coast. During Uther's time they grew in number and were constantly replenished by new immigrants from Germany. Buoyed by Uther's death and encouraged by the fighting among the Britons, they had ravaged much of the east, and the British kings were in complete flight. Arthur turned the kings around and with his army of Britons and Welsh faced the fierce Saxons near Badon. The Saxons stood on the hill with their fearsome shield wall and then marched down at Arthur's army. During the first day of battle, blood spilled freely, yet the Britons held and did not flee. The armies fought to a standstill, and the Saxons returned to the top of the hill. On the second day, bolstered by the fact that he was not defeated, Arthur and his great sword Excalibur threw himself against the Saxon wall. Fainwen watched as Arthur hewed down the Saxon soldiers and broke the shield wall. The remainder of the Britons set upon the wounded Saxons and killed them. Those that remained alive fled back to the shore. For thirty years the Saxons stayed in their Eastern villages near the Angles and Britain was in peace. During the struggle at Mont Badon, Fainwen killed many Saxons and afterward, King Arthur rewarded him with knighthood. Forever after he was one of the Fellowship of Arthur. When Leodegrance presented Arthur with the great round table, Fainwen sat at Camelot; one of the war chieftains.

Fainwen had seen it all. He had seen Arthur build his beautiful fortress Camelot near the River Cam and move between there and the old capital at Caerlon. He had seen the kingdoms of the Britons flourish under Arthur's reign. Yet after Merlin left, he also saw with sorrow how many of the Fellowship abandoned the protection of the Druid priests and priestesses and the protection of the Great Goddess in order to worship a God that promised little in this world.

Fainwen put his thoughts aside and pulled himself and his aching body to his feet. He called to his maid Nimenia. She was a beautiful young girl with flaming red hair that he had captured fighting in Ireland, and now she catered to all his needs. His manor house was in Wales, and the home he had near Camelot was too large for him alone. He never thought of himself as a homebody even when his wife was alive, and his children were small. He was a warrior who used his home just for rest. Now with his wife and children gone, he had sold his manor in Britain and maintained only a small apartment at Camelot for himself and Nimenia, who took care of him and his rooms.

His body ached and throbbed from the tournament and Nimenia fixed him a hot bath. She then bathed him and put soothing oils on his sore and tired muscles. There was to be a big dinner tonight in the great hall at Camelot celebrating the tournament and as one of the one hundred fifty of the Fellowship, he had to attend. After the bath and the oils, the pain abated a bit, she dried him, and he lay on his bed. Nimenia lay down by his side. As he aged, he no longer had the constant lust of his youth, and having her warm body lay next to him was enough. He quickly fell asleep but within some short hours, Nimenia woke him to attend the feast.

The feast was held in Arthur's great hall within his fortress at Camelot. The one hundred and fifty of the Fellowship (deaths had brought that number now closer to a hundred) sat at the main round table, the famous gift given to Arthur by his father-in-law Leodegrance. The King sat next to Guenevere and each of his main generals, the members of the Round Table Fellowship, like Fainwen, sat at his own seat. Many had their women by their side. The other knights and lesser soldiers and commanders sat at smaller tables placed throughout the hall. Servants scurried about the great dining hall bringing meat and bread and of course beer and wine. The soldiers of Camelot were served strong mead and for many the feasts were an occasion to get drunk. Often they became wild romps filled with lust. As Arthur turned more to the Christians, he tended to frown on the drunkenness and libertine behavior, but it was a tradition so the King allowed it to continue.

As they ate and drank, a herald sounded a great horn signaling an important arrival. All stopped to see who had arrived. The Herald brought forth two women and a young man and announced them. It was Arthur's two sisters, Queen Nicea, and Queen Morgana. Both were stunning beauties, even in middle age, and both were famous as necromancers and Druid priestesses. Their power was not as strong as Merlin's had been but both were renowned for their magic. The two sisters, who at various times, were either enemies or allies of their brother, walked forward and stood before the King. Standing beside them was a tall young man, about twenty. He was strong and handsome with dark hair and a dark beard and to Fainwen, he looked quite a bit like the King. The young man's eyes had a suspicious look, and they darted around the room as he stood before the great Fellowship.

Nicea brought the young man forward to face Arthur. The King spoke first, "My sister, how are things with you? You are welcome here at Camelot but be on your guard, I have now forbidden the old magic." He looked at the tall stranger next to her and asked, "Who is this young man?"

Nicea stepped forward and spoke while Morgana and the young stranger stood behind. "Brother we will abide by your rules and defer any use of magic. I come to Camelot not for myself but to present my son to you." She motioned for the young man to come forward. "This is Mordred," she said as she presented him to Arthur. She made no mention of who the boy's father was, but it was known that the beautiful Nicea, in the tradition of Druid priestesses, had many lovers. "He has come of age," she continued "and he has been trained well in my land as a warrior. I ask that he be made part of your fellowship. I know that many have died, and your great table has several empty seats. My son can ably fill one."

Arthur looked at the boy. He was powerfully built and had the appearance of a true knight. If his mother said that he was well-trained, then Arthur was certain that he was. On decisions such as these, the King usually conferred with some of the senior knights, especially Lancelot and Gawaine, but on this evening, Arthur acted alone. "Step forward lad and kneel before me," Arthur said as he drew out his sword, the famous Excalibur, from his scabbard. The boy did as he was instructed and Arthur stood and told him, "Mordred, I grant my sister's request. Do not disappoint me." He then raised Excalibur; "As King of the realm, I make you Sir Mordred and grant you a position in my Fellowship and a seat at the great table. Use your power wisely and for justice and peace. I dub you now Sir Mordred." Arthur then tapped him with Excalibur on each shoulder. "For tonight, Sir Mordred come sit by my side."

Arthur then turned to the whole banquet and announced loudly. "My fellow knights," the King said, "tonight I granted my nephew Mordred a seat in the Fellowship. It is his right by birth as my sister's son to be part of us."

Some knights grumbled, some even speaking out loudly. They felt that a position in the Fellowship had to be earned; to be a knight at the round table, one's reputation at warfare must be known. Yes, it was Arthur's right as King to grant a seat to Mordred, but the tradition at Camelot had been for him to take the counsel of his oldest knights.

Others, especially the newer knights, just shrugged and returned to their drinking and feasting. The general opinion was that Mordred's presence was of no concern to them.

Fainwen, at first had no opinion about the new Knight. The King had the right to grant his nephew a position in the Fellowship. Fainwen's hope was that Mordred would become worthy enough as a knight so that there would be no question about his membership.

As the months progressed, Arthur seemed to pull Mordred ever closer to him. Mordred began to be pushed into a leading position among the knights. Through his mother and aunt, he was a true follower of the old religion, the old magic, and the old ways. Many, who still believed in the Druids and the Great Goddess, began to look to him as a leader. On the other side, the knights who had accepted Christianity looked at him with great suspicion.

Then a rumor began to circulate among the people of Camelot. It started slowly and was often voiced in hushed whispers but as time progressed so did the rumor; Mordred was not Arthur's nephew but rather his son via an incestuous night the King had spent with his sister Nicea. The resemblance between Arthur and Mordred was astounding and most believed the rumor. The fact that Arthur did not deny it, nor ever address it, only made people believe it more. With each passing month, Mordred became closer and closer to the King, and his power grew. The factions also grew as those who believed in the old religion began to gather around Mordred as their leader.

To the traditional Britons, the fact that Mordred was born in incest, was not a good thing but not a terrible thing. The old ways understood the lust that men had and, as in Arthur's case, if a man's sister was not well-known to him, well these things could happen. To the Christians though, a child born of incest was the spawn of the devil, and the Bishop's looked at Mordred as pure evil.

Fainwen believed in the Great Goddess, and the magic of necromancers like Merlin, yet he held nothing against the Christian knights. Mordred's parentage did not trouble him. In fact, if Mordred were the King's son then he was the rightful heir since Arthur had no issue with his Queen Guenevere. The old time knights knew that Arthur had several sons scattered throughout Britain but had never acknowledged any of them. If he acknowledged Mordred their loyalty would then go to him.

Mordred was ambitious, but Fainwen thought no more evil that any other man. Through his mother Nicea and through his aunt Morgana, both Druid princesses, Mordred held fast to the old religion. The Christians, both for his birth in incest and for his beliefs in the old ways, held him to be the devil's child. Because of this, the factions of knights hardened, and the competition for loyalty was enlarged by the religious hatred each side had for the other.

Fainwen fell into a third faction that was loyal to Arthur and suspicious of both Mordred and the Christian bishops. This faction held many of the older warriors, including Lancelot, the greatest of the Fellowship. Lancelot and

Fainwen often spoke together of the decay they saw in the Fellowship. When Merlin disappeared much of the old ways left with him. The legend was that Merlin fell in love and his lust for the young and treacherous Nimue betrayed him. Fainwen and others though believed that a great magician and necromancer like Merlin was probably killed by his Christian enemies. With Merlin's guidance, Arthur's realm flourished. His kingdom paid homage to the Great Goddess Earth, and when necessary relied on Merlin's magic. Yet without Merlin, his great advisor and strength, Arthur aged and grew tired of fighting and diligence. He was seduced by the Christian clerics and their promise of eternal salvation. If Mordred was the son of Arthur's coupling with his sister, the Great Goddess and the old ways saw no great shame in this; yet the Christians saw it as the greatest sin and Arthur was tormented. He turned away from his wife, thought back on his first love Cuenemara, and ignored it as his Queen Guenevere dallied with his friend and greatest general Lancelot.

2

The Worthless Quest For
The Silver Chalice

As many of the older knights died, the rift between Christians and the followers of the old religion, widened.

Fainwen and his third faction watched from the outside and with sadness saw the decay of the Fellowship. Then came the worthless quest for the silver chalice; what the Christian knights called the Sangreal.

This odd quest began on an evening when the Fellowship again sat in the great hall feasting and drinking. In the middle of the festivities, a strange man entered. He had wild eyes and shaggy hair and was dressed like a Christian holy man. He walked through the great hall and stood before Arthur. The King called upon him to speak. The hall was too noisy, and most of the knights were too drunk to hear the stranger, but he spoke to those near him. Fainwen could see nothing, but others said that the stranger showed them the fleeting image of a silver chalice. "It is the cup that caught our Savior's blood as He bled on the cross," the holy man said, "and Joseph of Arimathea brought it to Britain. Only the purest knights can see it. It is hidden somewhere in Britain."

Before the King could answer the holy man, Galahad, Lancelot's son, acknowledged as second only to his father as a warrior, stood up to speak. He was a pure Christian and had the reputation of being the most virtuous of all the knights. The older warriors, such as Fainwen and Gawaine, often mocked him behind his back; holier than thou, they would joke.

"I will go after this holy relic and bring back the cup of our Savior," Galahad told the assembled crowd, most not listening. Arthur thought of Galahad's proposed quest and then heralded the whole hall to listen. As the noise in the great hall died down the King announced, "Let all my Fellowship go on this quest. It will be the crowning achievement of my reign to hold the great cup of our Savior."

One by one the Christian knights stood and vowed to search for the Sangreal. Strangely, Mordred, rather than opposing the quest stood silent, as if he knew it provided him with an opportunity to gain control. The knights in Mordred's circle hung back and did not dedicate themselves to this venture.

For Fainwen and Lancelot and their third faction, it put them in a strange position. They knew it was a worthless venture, a silly quest for a cup that might have held the blood of a long dead holy man. Still their loyalty to King Arthur forced them to take part as the senior members of the Fellowship.

As the weeks passed, one by one the younger Christian knights set out on this quest. There was a great air of excitement as groups left, not knowing where they were going, or what they were really looking for. With great fanfare the two purest and holiest knights, Galahad and Percival set out together.

Fainwen met secretly with his old comrade Lancelot. As the greatest of the Fellowship and with his son having proposed it, the mighty Breton was sworn to go on the quest. "Lancelot my friend," Fainwen told him, "we both know that this quest is worthless but we can't refuse to go; it is expected of us. I've decided to go to my lands in Wales; hunt, fish, rest and have some fun. Come with me. If, by some chance, we find this chalice, so much the better, but if we don't, then we had a good time."

Lancelot thought over this proposal but did not immediately reply. Fainwen knew that it was difficult for Lancelot to leave the Queen. The great warrior was trapped by love but tormented by guilt over his betrayal of his friend and commander Arthur. However, Lancelot was also required by his vow to go on the chalice hunt. Still to Lancelot, North Wales and some rest seemed like a good idea. "Fainwen my friend, I will go with you, but our plan must just be between us."

With more great fanfare, Fainwen and Lancelot set out. "We will bring back the chalice." Lancelot told the crowd that cheered them, but he and Fainwen knew that they were going to Wales to rest. They headed at first eastward so that no one would suspect their final destination.

At a crossroads, north of Camelot, they met Percival and Galahad. "We have traveled for weeks and seen nothing." Percival told them, "but our search will continue." Galahad was silent as if driven by a mad idea. Percival again spoke "We are told that the chalice is in the northeast in Saxon lands. It is dangerous, but for our Savior, we will go there. Join us Lancelot." Lancelot shook his head and said "Better that Fainwen and I go in a different direction. It is better to look in many places than for many to look together. Go with the Lord and good luck in your quest."

Percival and Galahad left them and headed further northeast while Lancelot and Fainwen continued on the road to North Wales. "Your son Galahad," Fainwen told his friend, "is obsessed with this quest. He is in his own world." Lancelot shook his head in agreement. "Fainwen, he is my son, but you know that I did not raise him. In truth, I hardly know him and most often do not even understand him. I know that he is pure in his belief for this Christian God. More power to him; he is certainly a fine warrior, not tested yet in battle, but it would be difficult for me to defeat him in a tournament." Lancelot had always refused to face his son, even in false combat.

As they traveled, Lancelot's colors and his shield and his armor were recognized by those they passed. Few had the courage to challenge the famous warrior so their passage into Wales was safe and uneventful. They sought out no adventures; this was to be a rest for them, a quiet respite for two warriors.

They arrived at Fainwen's Manor and his brother Fay greeted them. "Fainwen my brother, it is good to have you home after these many years, and it is an honor to welcome you, Lancelot." Fay was a landowner and not a warrior, and the manor house was decked out for comfort. Fainwen's brother prepared a feast for the two travelers with much food, wine, and beer. He also found two Welsh maids, young and fair to attend to their needs. Fay's wife, Conara, directed the maids in what to do. Conara was a true Welsh woman and understood what great warriors needed.

As the weeks passed the two Knights enjoyed their time. They hunted and fished and enjoyed the charms of their Welsh handmaidens. Both men grew a bit fat and loved the evenings, with their maidens and Fay's family, sitting by the fire and talking. Welsh singers and musicians hired by Fay serenaded them.

King Ryence learned that Fainwen and Lancelot were in North Wales and tried to set a trap for them. They were in a forest near Fay's manor and were relaxed and hunting, looking for a boar or for a stag. They had their swords and bows, but both were without armor. Suddenly they were set upon by a band of Ryence's men.

Ryence's henchmen were not prepared for two knights as skilled and ferocious as Lancelot and Fainwen. Even with no armor, they killed several of Ryence's assassins and escaped unharmed. Safely back at Fay's manor house, they sent a messenger to Ryence.

"We are here to enjoy ourselves in the lovely Welsh summer. Leave us alone or we will come for you." When Lancelot threatened, few would venture against him. King Ryence was no fool, and without the element of surprise, he had no desire to tangle with either Lancelot or Fainwen.

Free from any interference from Ryence, the two friends hunted and fished and enjoyed the Welsh maidens. They often talked of what the other knights from Arthur's court were doing on this silly chalice quest.

The summer turned to fall and then to winter and then back to spring. It was almost a year that they had been gone. "We must return," Lancelot said. He missed the queen. "We must decide on a story to tell at court," he told Fainwen.

Fainwen shrugged and said, "We will tell the Fellowship that we traveled about but found nothing. Only the pure can see the chalice and all of our comrades know that neither of us is pure." Lancelot smiled at this and agreed.

The two friends left North Wales and quickly returned to Camelot. Sadly they learned that many of the Fellowship had died on this strange and worthless quest and that no one had brought back the chalice. Some related the story that Galahad and Percival had found the silver cup and both had held the holy relic. After doing this, both had passed directly to heaven. Fainwen listened but shook his head. He knew that it was only a story sung by the Welsh bards, and Galahad and Percival must have died or perished in battle. Lancelot grieved for his son, but not as much for his loss, but for the fact that he hardly knew him.

As they had agreed upon, Fainwen and Lancelot told the others that they had traveled north and fought many strange knights and had many adventures. They had seen Galahad and Percival, but they had not come upon the chalice. For both, it was difficult to lie so openly, yet the rest they had in North Wales was good for the two.

Sadly Fainwen found the Fellowship was now in disarray. Many of the older knights had not returned from the Sangreal quest, and many now followed Mordred. Arthur replenished the seats at the great table by making many new knights. The King's brother-in-law, Constantis, brought a group from the court of King Leodegrance; young men and untested in battle.

Fainwen felt his age creeping up on him and looked with sorrow at the loss of both the soldiers and the loss of the great spirit that was Camelot. Yet he remained a warrior; it was the only life he understood.

3

On To Camlan And Death

Arthur's army was exhausted as they walked off the boats that had landed at the mouth of the Thames. It had almost been a half a year since the war with Lancelot led them to Little Britain. It had hurt Fainwen, not physically, but in his spirit, to fight in a war against his close friend. Still, Fainwen above all was a loyal warrior and fought for Arthur whatever his personal feelings. Lancelot had betrayed his King and liege lord by having an affair with the Queen, yet Arthur would not have fought him and would have gladly forgiven them both. Arthur was tired and weary from his years of ruling and years of warfare and had knowingly ignored Guenevere's dalliance with his greatest general and closest friend. Arthur's mind often drifted back to his first love, the common Welsh maiden Cuenamara, whom after he became King, he was forbidden to marry. Guenevere was as beautiful as any woman in the realm, but the marriage had been arranged as an alliance with her father Leodegrance, and she came into Arthur's life when his greatest lust was abated. He never gave her the attention that her beauty and spirit merited. If she needed the warmth of a younger man like Lancelot, and it was in secret and not embarrassing to the throne, then Arthur understood. In his youth, he had also dallied with many married women.

Mordred and Gawaine, each for their own reasons, pushed and urged Arthur to defend his honor against Lancelot. As Fainwen knew well, Lancelot was a great warrior, but still just a man. He was trapped by love, like Merlin and so many others before him had been. The Queen was also a prisoner of her passion for the great Breton, but she was tormented by her adultery. She turned even more to Christianity because of her guilt.

When their affair became known, Lancelot fled Camelot, and the Queen was to be burned for her treachery. Lancelot could not desert her, saved her from the fire and carried her off to his homeland Little Britain. He abandoned his lands and castle, the New Joyous Garde, in Great Britain and brought her to Brittany. Now although together with her great love, the Queen was crippled by her guilt and turned away from Lancelot.

Arthur brought his army to Brittany and left Mordred as regent in Great Britain. Lancelot surrendered the Queen to Arthur, who sent Guenevere back to Camelot, pardoned but shamed. Even though the Queen was returned, Gawaine, always jealous of Lancelot, pressured Arthur to avenge his brothers who had been killed by the Breton. Arthur reluctantly laid siege to Lancelot's castle.

Lancelot though, would not fight Arthur and kept his army within Old Joyous Garde. Although Fainwen knew that Lancelot and his army from Fenwick could probably defeat Arthur, Lancelot allowed the King to continue the siege.

On Arthur's part, it was a half-hearted siege. Arthur would not have fought his friend and as the months passed he wished only for a rapprochement. Lancelot's brother Banwick, the regent of Little Britain, constantly tried to arrange a truce. Arthur might have poisoned the wells or starved the army at Old Joyous Garde but did none of that, and Lancelot would not fight outside of the castle except on two occasions. He fought personal combat against Gawaine and both times held back. Fainwen knew that he could have easily killed the arrogant Gawaine, who hated him for killing his brothers Agravaine and Gareth, yet Lancelot only held Gawaine at bay.

As they camped in Brittany in front of Old Joyous Garde they received the news from Britain; Mordred had seized the throne. He told the court that Arthur was dead and then tried to force Guenevere to be his wife. To avoid Mordred's advances she fled to a nunnery in Almsbury.

Arthur and his forces began their sad voyage back to Britain to fight against Mordred and their own brethren. They were tired, and many had died of sickness, and many more were malnourished. Mordred's army attacked them near the mouth of the Thames. Mordred, hearing of the bad condition of Arthur's troops, expected an easy victory. He also believed that his mother Nicea provided him with strong magic that would help to defeat the old king.

Yet at the seashore Arthur's forces fought like madmen and drove Mordred's army backwards. Fainwen killed three young knights that he did not know and then hacked away at the Welsh archers that accompanied Mordred's host.

Mordred brought reinforcements, but Arthur chased Mordred's forces across Britain. The two armies were now arrayed against each other on the plain of Camlan near the River Cam. Mordred had the stronger force, with more knights and more archers, yet Arthur occupied the higher ground and the more advantageous position. Fainwen sadly knew that this will be the last great battle of the Fellowship, win or lose.

Arthur's brother-in-law Constantis met with Mordred. They arranged a truce since Arthur, weary and heartsick, wanted to avoid more bloodshed. The two armies, Arthurs" in the red and green of the Pendragons, and Mordred's, in the black and grey of Nicea, faced each other on the Plain of Camlann while Constantis and Mordred tried to work out a settlement.

Fainwen never knew what started the battle. The legend is that a knight drew his sword to kill a serpent, and that started the hostilities, but most in both armies knew nothing except to draw their own swords and begin fighting. The clash of metal on metal was like a thunderclap and Fainwen set quickly on two of Mordred's soldiers. He had been in many battles, yet this was like none he had ever seen.

4

The Fall of Camelot
Fainwen's Final Sorrow

Fainwen began to pull himself to his feet. He was shaky; the blow from the mace had split his helmet and knocked him senseless. How long he had been out, he couldn't tell, yet he knew now that he was alive. He remembered that the sword blade had pierced his shoulder and as he tried to stand, both his head and shoulder throbbed with pain. He reached to his shoulder underneath his mail shirt, and the blood had dried. His own sword had been shattered in the battle, and he saw it lying broken by his side.

As he got onto his knees, he saw his kinsman Clonwyn, from the same town in Wales, laying dead. A mace had split Clonwyn's helmet, and Fainwen saw part of his kinsman's brains next to the bloody head. Clonwyn's squire, Casademus lay close by; a fatal sword wound clearly visible in his chest. Fainwen's own squire was nowhere around.

He surveyed the battlefield. There seemed to be no further fighting on this part of the river plain, yet he did not know the outcome of the battle. The ground, as far as he could see in all directions, was strewn with the bodies of dead knights and soldiers and the corpses of fallen horses. He saw many of his friends, clad like him in the red and green of Arthur's forces, bloody and dead near him, yet he also saw many he did not know, clad in the black and grey of Mordred's army. The ground was red and brown with the blood of the many fallen knights, and the River Cam, alongside which the battle had been fought, flowed red with blood.

In the distance on the far hill, above the plain of the River Cam, he saw the tent of King Arthur still standing.

Arthur's banner, the banner of the Pendragons, still flew. It had not fallen. He thought with some relief that the battle must be won for our side. As a soldier for so many years, the outcome of the battle meant everything to Fainwen. Now on his feet and with his mind somewhat clearer, he could see a group of knights standing by the tent and here and there a survivor standing on the battlefield.

His shoulder hurt and his arm and head ached yet he started to walk uneasily towards Arthur's tent. He would need a sword; his own sword shattered and his scabbard was empty. Fainwen turned over one of the mortally wounded knights who lay on the ground below his feet. It was Sir Gamnyn, a newly made knight, no more than a boy. His head like Clonwyn's had been split, and his brain lay partially outside of his body. The young face, smooth and still beardless, looked like he was sleeping calmly. It was such a shame for one to die so young, not even to have tasted many battles and many adventures. Fainwen's own sons, Fen and Lors, had died in battles, but they had fought in many. A warrior, Fainwen believed, must taste both victory and defeat for his death to mean something. Fainwen reached down and took Gamnyn's sword from his hand and then unhooked the scabbard from the dead boy's waist and let his own drop.

Sheathing the sword in the new scabbard, he then continued walking towards the tent.

A hundred paces further on he came upon Caias, the squire to Sir Benlan, one of the hundred-fifty of the Table Fellowship. Caias was on his knee's weeping; Benlan's body, bloody and lifeless lay next to him.

"Caias, is your master dead?" Fainwen asked.

"Yes," said the squire as he wept some more.

"What of the battle? Has Arthur prevailed?" Fainwen asked the weeping squire.

Caias hung his head and answered, "All is lost, and all is won." He briefly looked up the hill at Arthur's pavilion and then said, "Arthur lies mortally wounded in his tent. His reign is over, but he slew Mordred and Mordred's army has fled north."

"Is Arthur still alive?" Fainwen asked as if pleading. Perhaps he could see the great king that he had served for so long, one more time.

"I don't know but I know that he is dying," Caias told him.

Fainwen hurried as best he could in his painful state towards the tent of the King. He realized that this was certainly the end of the Fellowship and perhaps the end of the Britons. It was only Arthur that stopped the Saxons from swallowing all of Britain. Big parts of the east were now lost to the Angles and were called Anglia. Further north on the eastern coastline were mostly Saxon villages and the Britons were living further west inland. Only Wales, Cornwall, and Scotland seemed safe. The fortified Roman towns, like Londinium, that had survived the departure of Roman troops and still stood, had many Saxons living in them mixed with Britons. Fainwen's own lands in North Wales were only safe because of the high mountains.

As he walked through the blood-drenched battlefield, strewn with fallen knights and soldiers, he passed some priests praying over men. He watched the clerics in their black robes giving last rites and Fainwen could only look in sorrow and regret. He thought ruefully how it was Arthur's turn to the Christians in Londinium and away from the magic of the Druid priestesses and priests that led to the downfall of Camelot and the downfall of the Fellowship. When Merlin lived, Arthur listened to the old necromancer, and his magic and the magic of the Great Goddess kept Arthur's kingdom safe. From the great stone circles at Stonehenge, to the rock temples in the Welsh mountains, the allegiance of the Britons to the old ways had been everywhere. The Christians though promised a salvation beyond this mortal existence, and it seduced many of the

Celts. When Merlin followed Nimue and never returned, Arthur began to listen to the Christian bishops. As the king turned to this strange God Jesus, the protection of Great Goddess, and the protection of Merlin's magic fell away, and the Fellowship began to fall apart.

As he struggled towards the king's tent, his body continued to throb with pain yet Fainwen had lived through the great battle and seen the end. At the crest of the hill, he came upon a small group of knights gathered about a fire on the outside of the king's pavilion. So many of the older knights that he had fought alongside for these many years had died or been killed, and Fainwen did not know these younger soldiers. They did not recognize him either, but since he wore the red and green, they let him pass and ignored him.

Fainwen entered Arthur's tent. A small lamp burned and cast a sorrowful light while the wounded King Arthur lay on a cot, his bloodied body in a heap. The King's breath could be heard but the breathing was labored, and Arthur did not move. There was no sword by the King's side; the great Excalibur was gone. Arthur was being attended by Sir Bedivere and Sir Lothyn, who stood next to the cot. Every so often, Bedivere wiped Arthur's brow and poured a bit of cold water into his mouth. From the heavy wounds on his body, and the labored breathing, Fainwen could tell that Arthur was lost. Now it was just time until the great King passed from this world to the next. Sir Bedivere turned and acknowledged Fainwen. He winced and shook his head knowingly, indicating that there was no hope. "Fainwen," Bedivere asked, "help us carry him to the river. He still breathes slightly, and we have a ship to carry him to the priestesses at Avalon."

Fainwen and several of the younger knights carried the motionless king down the hill to the River Cam. A small boat with three Druid priestesses clad in flowing dresses waited. They placed Arthur in a soft bed on the deck of the vessel, and Bedivere, ever faithful, tried to follow. One of the women stopped him. "He must go alone," she said, "our lady at Avalon will do what the magic allows." Bedivere went back to the shore and stood with Lothyn and Fainwen. The group sadly watched the boat carry the King away. Fainwen knew that Arthur was surely dead and the dream of his reign and the rule of Camelot, that Fainwen had lived with for most of his life, was over.

"What now?" Fainwen asked Bedivere.

Bedivere shook his head. "Life will be different my friend. Arthur's brother-in-law Constantis, son of King Leodegrance, is now in command. By Arthur's wishes, he will be anointed King by the Bishop in Londinium. He has taken the small force that has survived back to Camelot, perhaps to raise a new army to chase Mordred's remnants."

Fainwen listened. In his mind, he had no choice but to follow the new king. "Bedivere I have known no life but that of a soldier. I guess I will go to find Constantis."

Bedivere again shook his head. "Do what you must Fainwen, but I will return to my own lands in the west and try to live in peace. Things are now so much more complicated. While we fought in Little Britain against Lancelot, the Saxons began to pillage the east. Constantis will pursue Morded's followers to consolidate the kingdom, but it is the Saxons that are now the true danger."

"That may be true Bedivere but what life do I have but that of a soldier?" Saying that, he left Bedivere, who stood and watched the King's deathbed boat floating in the distance.

Just as he had found a sword among the many dead knights, Fainwen found an abandoned horse among the many riderless steeds wandering the field. He mounted and began his ride back to Camelot. There was nothing else for him to do but join Constantis and continue to fight Mordred. King Ryence controlled Fainwen's Welsh town so returning home to Wales, after so many years fighting alongside Arthur and the Fellowship, was not an option.

Fainwen began to ride towards Camelot to join Constantis. As he rode, the sadness of seeing the dying Arthur carried away to Avalon pressed heavy on his heart. Upon reaching the main east-west road, a good Roman road that had survived all the British wars and all the neglect since the Romans left, he found it crowded with refugees. Both rich and poor, they were fleeing westward, away from the rampaging Saxons. With the Britons in civil war and disarray, Saxon strength was renewed, and the German invaders were once again pushing inward to the British heartland. The Saxons had been pillaging far in from their shoreline strongholds, and their deprivations were extensive. Their strategy, besides conquest, was to scare the Britons into submission. Fainwen saw fear and urgency on the faces of the refugees, a fear he had not seen since Arthur defeated the Saxon's at Mont Badon thirty years before.

Seeing the flood of refugees, and realizing the danger the Saxons were bringing, Fainwen changed directions and hurried further east to the town of Mantorious, where his daughter, son-in-law, and grandchildren lived. His daughter was the only one of his children left alive, His sons had died. They had been warriors like Fainwen, joined him at Camelot and were lost in battles over the years. His son-in-law, Maneboris, was a wealthy landowner near the old Roman city. As Fainwen headed towards the town, he contended with the flock of Britons fleeing in the other direction.

Arriving near the city, but still away from Maneboris's holdings, he stopped on a hill high above the town. From this hilltop position, he could see Mantorious in the distance and sadly he saw that a Saxon banner flew from the city walls. From his high position, he also saw that many of the smaller villages that surrounded the once proud Roman town had been burned.

He rode carefully around the town, watching closely for Saxon soldiers, and went to his son-in-law's estate. He found the manor house burned and his son-in-law impaled on a stake outside of the main gate, a method the Saxons used to scare their foes. He could only assume that his daughter and grandchildren were carried off by the Saxons. Fainwen, stoic as always, could do nothing more, so once again he turned to the south and west.

Back again near the battlefield at Camlan, Fainwen came upon Lancelot's army. Despite their own struggle, the great warrior Lancelot had come to Arthur's rescue. Sadly, he had arrived too late. Fainwen and Lancelot had been friends since the great Breton had arrived at Camelot and among the

Fellowship during recent years, they were among the few who were still warriors. They lived for battle and not for quests and silly adventures. The Welsh love to sing, and their troubadours and singers had built legends and songs around Arthur's court, even as Arthur's Fellowship still lived. Lancelot was the hero of many of many of these songs, yet Fainwen knew the real Lancelot; the Lancelot who knew the danger of the battlefield but lived it anyway. The Lancelot, who despite his hopeless love for Guenevere, was a hardened soldier who put little stock in his reputation and had little time for frivolous adventures. Like Fainwen, he did not pursue the holy chalice, despite what the legends and troubadours sang.

Lancelot's soldiers took Fainwen to their general, where Fainwen told his friend of the battle at Camlann, and wept as he related the sad news of Arthur's death.

"What of Guenevere?" Lancelot asked, forever tied to his love for the queen.

"Still at Camelot, as far as I know," Fainwen told him. "Mordred attempted to take her as his wife, but she resisted him."

Fainwen now went with Lancelot's army to Camelot. He had no personal plan, his world had been destroyed, and so he followed his soldier's heart and became part of his friend Lancelot's force. Much of the populace of Camelot had fled, pressed on one side by the marauding Saxons and on the other still fearful from the north of Mordred's survivors. Constantis had tried to rally a new army, now more concerned with the Saxons than in pursuing Mordred's men. Lancelot's army was welcomed at Camelot and Lancelot met with the harried Constantis, who was not really up to the task of replacing Arthur. Lancelot, more for Arthur's memory than for what his heart desired, pledged support to the Britons under Constantis. Lancelot's thoughts though were always on the queen. "Where is Queen Guenevere?" he asked Constantis.

The leader answered him, ignoring Lancelot's role in all that had happened. "She felt ashamed of the part she played in the fall of her husband. She has gone to the Almsbury nunnery at Brixton."

Fainwen knew that the British bards and troubadours in their songs and epics had made Lancelot the greatest of the British heroes. In these epics, Lancelot had become more than a man. He was a mythic figure that stood above the rest of humanity. Yet Fainwen knew Lancelot well. He had fought beside him for the twenty years since Lancelot left Little Britain to join Arthur's Fellowship. He knew Lancelot not as a superman, nor a god, but as a tough soldier, a battle-hardened warrior who somehow fell in love with Guenevere and betrayed his friend and commander Arthur. He saw Lancelot torn between the old ways and the Christianity that Guenevere had adopted, and he saw that the guilt that Guenevere felt had been transferred to Lancelot. Earlier in his life Lancelot had easily been with any married woman he desired. That was his right as a great general, and he felt no guilt. Yet with Guenevere there were two great sins; one the sin of adultery that her Christian beliefs pushed forward but more than that was the sin of betrayal of his friend and liege lord Arthur.

"Fainwen my friend," Lancelot said. "Come with me to this nunnery. I can do nothing, but I must see the lady." Fainwen agreed and rode with Lancelot to see the fallen queen.

Guenevere, once a proud and confident queen, and a beauty beyond almost all maidens, was racked with guilt over her love for Lancelot. She believed that the collapse of Camelot was her fault, and it was God's punishment for her transgressions. At the nunnery at Brixton, she removed herself from the world and took a vow as a nun. Because of her position as Queen, the Bishop at Brixton appointed her the mother superior of the nunnery.

Lancelot and Fainwen arrived at the nunnery where they were announced to the Prioress. They were led to a small side garden where Guenevere, dressed in a nun's habit met with them. Her face had aged terribly, and the religious garb hid whatever beauty was left. Lancelot though still looked on her with love in his eyes. Fainwen stood behind and off to the side as Lancelot approached the only woman, beyond his mother Elaine, who he had loved. Fainwen watched them speak but heard nothing. However, he saw that Guenevere held her former lover off at a distance. Her manner was brusque, and Lancelot appeared crushed, more like a scolded puppy than a great general. She spoke to him quickly and dismissed her former champion.

Lancelot said nothing and he and Fainwen left the nunnery together in silence. Fainwen, through his own sadness, saw the sadness in the great knight as the rest of Lancelot's world was lost to him.

At a spot a mile from the nunnery Lancelot stopped and dismounted. He sat down on a tree stump, and the famous hero wept like a child. Fainwen also dismounted and stood off a bit, leaving his comrade to suffer his grief in peace. Lancelot then called to his friend to sit with him.

"Fainwen my friend, my life is over. I have decided that I will also take a vow and go to a monastery to live out my days." With great regret etched on his scarred warrior's face, he then told Fainwen, "All is spoiled, and I am the evil that caused the rot."

Fainwen, who had known no life other than a soldier's life, and had always managed to press onward, no matter what evil had been thrust on him, tried to dissuade the great general. "We are warriors Lancelot," Fainwen told his shattered friend, "and warriors must fight to live. I have lost everything also, our pasts are over, but we must go forward. There is no other way."

As they sat on the tree stump, a messenger arrived from Lancelot's army. "My Lord," the messenger began, "an urgent note has come from your brother Banwyn." Banwyn reigned as king in Little Britain since Lancelot had joined Arthur's Fellowship in Great Britain. He was the younger son of Kin Ban, who died in the fire that Lancelot survived. The messenger continued. "The Gauls are pressing on Brittany from the east while the Bretons are being attacked by the Norsemen from the north. Your brother asks that you come to his aid."

King Ban and Arthur had defeated the Gauls years before, and Little Britain had been safe. For years, the Bretons had also been able to fight off the Norsemen, whose cousins, the Danes, were pillaging the north of Great Britain.

Now with Great Britain in turmoil, Little Britain could not stop its enemies.

A fierce look now came into Lancelot's eyes. The note from his brother had reignited his soldier's spirit and resolve and had changed his mind. "Fainwen," he told his companion, "you are right. A soldier lives to fight, and I must return to my home in Fenwick to protect the Bretons.

Fainwen's family was dead; Wales belonged to Arthur's enemies, and much of Arthur's realm was now threatened by Saxons. Constantis was weak. Fainwen decided to cast his lot with Lancelot and go with the Breton's army to Brittany. Fainwen was old, but he knew no other life so he decided to die fighting for Lancelot.

Fainwen returned with Lancelot to Camelot and over the objections of Constantis, Lancelot led his army away. Moving eastward they passed Londinium that now was in the hands of Britons and Saxons who had become Christians. Fainwen, with some bitterness, again thought that it was the Christians that brought Arthur down.

Lancelot's ships—that had carried his army across the Channel from Brittany—had waited for them and his forces re-crossed the water near the mouth of the Thames. On the sea, Fainwen looked back on Great Britain and his mind drifted to better times when Merlin guided the kingdom.

With Merlin's guidance, Arthur's realm flourished yet without his great advisor and strength Arthur grew tired of fighting and diligence. He was seduced by the Christian Bishops and their promise of eternal salvation.

Arriving at Banwyn's castle, Olde Joyous Garde, in Brittany, Lancelot met with his brother and then led his army northward to confront the Norsemen, called Normans by the Bretons. They were harassing the north of Little Britain, and Banwyn told Lancelot that they were the greatest threat to the Breton lands.

The Normans fought much like the Saxons with a strong shield wall. Lancelot with all the ferocity he had garnered through years as a soldier and warrior had his troops attack the Normans and their shield wall head on. Guided forward by Lancelot they hacked the Normans down. The Norman army fled, and the northern portion of Brittany was safe. In the battle, a Norman sword sliced through Fainwen's calf and after so many years on the battlefield he was crippled. Only able to hobble, he could no longer follow the forces of his new general into battle, so he had to sit idly in the court in Fenwick as Lancelot continued his campaigns.

The great knight, without Fainwen, then led his army eastward to fight the Gauls. Hearing of Lancelot's slaughter of the Normans, the Gauls put up only minimal resistance and fled back to their homeland. For a time, under the protection of Lancelot, Brittany was again safe. With his brother as King at Fenwick, Lancelot built a Fellowship of warriors at Joyous Gard, much like Arthur had built in Camelot.

Fainwen could not return to Great Britain; there was nothing for him in his own homeland. He had fought well with Lancelot, and though crippled, Fainwen begged to join the new Fellowship. Lancelot granted him his wish. Lancelot was victorious, but the sadness in him did not die. His Fellowship, like that of Arthur's, would die with its leader.

Fainwen, now old and crippled, sat at the court in Fenwick and watched as events unfolded. He had survived all that life had thrown at him, but he knew that his time was near its end.

Contributors

Art by Jim Sanders

Ben Fine

Dr. Ben Fine is a mathematician and professor at Fairfield University in Connecticut in the United States. He is a graduate of the MFA program at Fairfield University and is the author of twelve books (ten in mathematics, one on chess, one a political thriller) as well over 130 research articles. In addition he has published several short stories as well as a novella about pirates.

His memoir, told in interwoven stories is *Tales from Brighton Beach: A Boy Grow in Brooklyn* and details growing up in Brighton Beach, a seaside neighborhood on the southern tip of Brooklyn during the 1950's and 1960's. Brighton Beach was unique and set apart from the rest of New York City both in character and in time.

The present story is part of of a lifelong fascination with being a hero-cowboys, pirates and knights. In his mind, he has always been Sir Lancelot.

Cynthia Morrison

Cynthia Morrison B.A. resides in south Florida where she is a writer, artist, stage combat director, and an award winning playwright.

She is a graduate of the Burt Reynolds Institute. Her plays have appeared Off Broadway in New York, Washington D.C. and Internationally in London England.

Cynthia's works tend to lean towards historic content; although she also specializes in works that speak against the suppression of women. She has since retired from sport, where she had reigned as a three time Women's International Jousting Champion.

DJ Tyrer

DJ is the person behind Atlantean Publishing and has been widely published in anthologies and magazines in the UK, USA, and elsewhere, including Disturbance (Laurel Highlands), Tales of the Black Arts (Hazardous Press), Amok!, Stomping Grounds and Ill-considered Expeditions (all April Moon Books), History and Mystery, Oh My! (Mystery & Horror LLC), Destroy All Robots (Dynatox Ministries), and Sorcery & Sanctity: A Homage to Arthur Machen (Hieroglyphics Press), and in addition, has a novella available in paperback and on the Kindle, The Yellow House (Dunhams Manor).

DJ Tyrer's website is at http://djtyrer.blogspot.co.uk/

The Atlantean Publishing website is at:

http://atlanteanpublishing.blogspot.co.uk/

Michelle Monagin

Michelle has been writing since she was fourteen years old, and writes primarily Science Fiction and Fantasy.

Her writing has appeared in several anthologies. You can follow Michelle's blog at:

http://www.michellemmonagin.com

Sammi Cox

Sammi lives in the UK and spends her time writing and making things. She has been interested in history, archaeology and the natural world since she was a child.

However, it is tales of myth, magic and folklore that have captured her heart, and where she finds the greatest inspiration.

Shane Porteous

Shane is a mastery of the legendary 77 donut devouring technique. He lives in a place of strange dreams and even stranger reality.

A lifelong writer, he has an immense passion for the fantastical and prides himself on being alterative, and if possible, original with his storytelling. He has been published both traditionally and independently.

The single guarantee he gives with his novels is not whether you will like or hate them, but he guarantees you will remember them.

A Note from the Publisher

How to Thank a Contributor

Dear Reader,

Everyone at Zimbell House Publishing would like to thank you for reading *Tournament Games*. If you would like to thank a particular contributor, the best way is to leave a review for them. You may do so by leaving one on our Goodreads page, under the *Tournament Games* title, by using the link below:

http://www.goodreads.com/ZimbellHousePublishing
and be sure to mention the contributor directly.

Why leave a review? Reviews help budding authors build their credibility in the book industry. By posting a review on Goodreads, you help other readers find new authors they may wish to follow, and you never know, your review may end up on an author's website one day.

Friend us on Goodreads:

https://www.goodreads.com/ZimbellHousePublishing

Visit our website:

http://www.ZimbellHousePublishing.com

Follow us on Twitter:

http://twitter.com/ZimbellHousePub